They move across the field in a staggered line, weapons drawn, the overgrown grass and weeds nearly to their waists. The fog moves with them as they negotiate the uneven terrain, slowly, cautiously, the darkness deepening with each step they take. The scarecrows watch from their wooden crosses, some nailed, some tied with rotting lengths of rope, manlike ghouls in old and torn denim overalls and decayed work shirts, hands of straw protruding from the sleeves like talons, legs dangling, vanishing into the tall grass. With badly worn, stuffed and filthy burlap sacks for heads, their mouths are stiff grim lines of worn leather thread sewn into the fabric in a disturbing criss-cross pattern, their eyes sunken black holes, as if the sockets have been long-since picked clean.

"Notice anything about those scarecrows?"

"There are six of them. Six scarecrows."

"So?"

"There are six of us."

Kingdom of Shadows original publication by Altar 13—2010
Sorcerer original publication by Delirium Books—October 2010
ISBN 978-1-949914-78-8

For information address Crossroad Press at 141 Brayden Dr., Hertford, NC 27944
A Mcabre Ink Production - MXvew Ink is an imprint of Crossroad Press.
www.crossroadpress.com

First edition

KINGDOM OF SHADOWS

&

SORCERER

NOVELLA DOUBLE SHOT #3

BY GREG F. GIFUNE

CONTENTS

KINGDOM OF SHADOWS

"Shape without form, shade without colour,
Paralysed force, gesture without motion;
Those who have crossed
With direct eyes, to death's other Kingdom
Remember us —if at all —not as lost Violent souls, but only
As the hollow men The stuffed men."

—T.S. Eliot, *"The Hollow Men"*

1

The van rockets through darkness, swaying and bouncing along the bumpy road. The breakneck speed no longer seems necessary, but everyone is preoccupied and still racing on adrenaline and fear. For several minutes there is relative silence, but Carbone resumes his screaming and writhing about, knees pulled in close to his chest as his bloody hands clutch desperately at the mangled flesh that was once his stomach.

"Hang on, bro." Snow pokes his head up between the front bucket seats and looks to Rooster. "We need to get him to a hospital!"

"He's already dead," Rooster tells him.

Between screams, Carbone wheezes and literally cries for his mother.

"Christ," Nauls groans, "his intestines, I—I can see his fucking intestines!"

Landon, a white-knuckled grip on the steering wheel, glances quickly at the rearview then increases speed despite the rough terrain.

"Slow down," Starker says, his deep voice booming from his position at the rear of the van. "This ride dies, you die with it."

"Whatever," Landon says indignantly.

"We can't just let him bleed out," Snow says.

Rooster watches the darkness through the windshield wash over them like renegade waves. He's always liked Carbone, and knows he and Snow are best friends, but they're miles from any hospital. Game over.

"Goddamn it!" Snow leans closer. "You hear me?" Rooster looks back at Snow. "Stay with him, all right?" he says evenly. "Don't let him die alone."

After several seconds, reality sinks in, and with a defeated nod, Snow disappears into the back.

"Where the hell are we?" Rooster asks Landon.

"No clue, been following these country roads for miles now." He nervously paws perspiration from his face with the back of his free hand. "You wanted the middle of nowhere. You got it."

Rooster is about to tell him to slow down when the van comes to a sudden stop. Everyone lurches forward and Carbone screams again.

Before them, fog rolls across a field of weeds and overgrown grass. In the distance, an old farmhouse sits in the darkness and mist. The moon is full but obscured by clouds, scarcely illuminating a series of hideous scarecrows nailed to rotting wooden crosses scattered throughout the property.

"What is this place?" Nauls asks. Landon squints. "Looks abandoned."

With a final gagging cough, Carbone vomits blood and bile and dies on the floor of the van in a pool of his own excrement and urine.

What they don't understand is that his death is far more merciful than anything they'll ever know.

Distant screams echoed in his mind like the sudden screech of tires. He had no idea where he was, but his first conscious thought was that something was chasing him. The sheer curtains billowed, danced before him like smoke. It seemed as if he'd been watching them for hours, though he couldn't be sure. He'd been asleep, hadn't he? Below, city streets were awakening, coming alive as the sun slowly rose over a horizon of brick and steel. It was far too cold outside for the windows to be open, but he assumed Gaby had opened them at some point during the night.

Rooster sat up in bed and swung his feet onto the chilly floor. He leaned forward, face in his hands. It felt like an eternity since his old life had ended. Yet there was a disconnect between the here-and-now and the past, as if one or the other wasn't quite true, falling closer to waking nightmares than reality. Even the night he and his old crew pulled their last caper was such a blur he often had difficulty piecing his scant memories into anything coherent. But for Carbone, he and the others got away. He knew that much. He remembered the final score and leaving that way of life behind him. For a long while the past had stayed buried, forgotten, perhaps even consciously ignored, but over the last few weeks, flashes of memories had returned, mostly in tiny bits and pieces. He couldn't be sure, but Rooster suspected that's what had started the awful headaches he'd been suffering from of late, his continued attempts to remember in more detail.

The farmhouse…he remembered that dark farmhouse they'd ended up at to split the take. He remembered the moon that night…and scarecrows…horrible scarecrows. He remembered them too.

And then, like a reel of film that had run its course, the memories stopped, returning his mind to an equally unsettling darkness.

Though tall, thin and wiry, with angular features and a receding swath of buzzed-down brown hair, the nickname he'd had since high school still fit, but his body was slowing with age, and for the first time he'd begun to notice it, to really feel it. He moved his hand up behind his neck and squeezed, rubbing down to his trapezius muscles. He sported the remains of a tan, his skin a deep bronze, the veins and muscles in his arms and legs defined and strong. He patted his stomach. Not quite the six-pack it had once been, but flat and tight, nothing to be ashamed of.

A breeze blew through the windows, disturbing the curtains once again.

This time they were shredded and filthy with dirt and blood, dangling there like sheets of slashed flesh.

Rooster looked away, clenched shut his eyes.

When he opened them the curtains were back to normal, but everything felt askew now, as if something or someone had entered the bedroom without his consent. He stood up, glanced around, eyes panning the room.

Nothing…no one…

A chill licked his spine. "Are you all right?"

He turned to the doorway to find Gaby standing there bundled in a robe, dark hair mussed and the look on her face a mixture of horror and concern. "You were screaming."

Rooster grabbed his Marlboros and a lighter from the nightstand, lit a cigarette and blew a stream of smoke at the windows. "I wasn't even asleep."

Her expression softened, and she leaned against the doorframe with a sigh. "Yeah, I know. You never sleep anymore, not really."

"The windows..."

"I opened them." She hugged herself. "Fresh air's good for you."

Rooster drew another drag, coughed it out. "It's freezing."

Her brown eyes—so dark they were nearly black—sparkled in place of a smile. "It's good for the soul."

"Nothing can live long in the cold," he mumbled.

Gaby nodded but said nothing.

Shadows lay across the room like fallen spirits. Rooster stepped through them, approaching the windows with caution. A cold and dreary day stared back, the sky gray and overcast, the streets beyond the housing project courtyard dirty and cracked, cold and still mostly abandoned; the buildings in the neighborhood old and rundown, many of them condemned and long forgotten. *Such a bleak city,* he thought. Even where bustling life should've thrived, there was only emptiness, decay and an overwhelming sense of hopelessness. He looked back over his shoulder at Gaby. It seemed to him her name should've been Grace, since she was like a savior, the only consistently good and beautiful presence in what had become an otherwise murky existence. When it was just the two of them and they held each other close in the night, the fear in him subsided. In those moments he felt alive again, perhaps even happy, but like all else he'd once believed in, Gaby would eventually leave him and he'd be alone again in the darkness with his nightmares and the awful echo of faraway screams...

"What are you thinking about?" she asked.

"Your name."

"My name?"

"It's pretty. Gabrielle."

"I didn't realize it interested you." She smiled as if letting him in on a secret. "You've never mentioned it before."

"Never really thought about it until now, I guess."

"Its origin is Hebrew," she explained. "Most people don't know that."

"What does it mean?"

"God is my might."

Their eyes met, and for a moment he was lost in them, their depth and beauty. He knew her so well, and yet in many ways she seemed unfamiliar. How could that be? He focused on the writing table beneath the windows, the bills scattered about it.

"I better get in the shower," Gaby said. "Don't want to be late for work."

Right, he thought. *Someone's got to earn some money around here.*

"I'll find something," he promised. "There's been some talk that big warehouse facility over on Dover Street's hiring."

"That place gives me the creeps," she said. "What do they warehouse there anyway?"

"I don't know. All I heard is they need some extra hands to unload trucks. It's temporary but steady work for a week or more. Word is they're only hiring a few people, so I want to get there early."

"What about the phone calls?"

Fear rose from deep inside him. "What about them?"

Gaby came closer, padding across the chilly pockmarked floor in her bare feet, nails painted blood red and a dainty gold ankle bracelet adorned with tiny bells jingling as she moved. "It's obviously important. He's called at least half a dozen times, and at all hours, too." She slid up behind him and wrapped her hands around his waist. She smelled vaguely of freshly cut flowers, and her breath caressed the back of his neck in slow, sensual intervals. "He says he knows you."

"That was a long time ago."

"Are you going to call him back?" When he didn't answer she leaned into him and brushed her lips against his ear. "He sounds so *frightened,* the man on the phone."

With a sad smile, Rooster flicked his cigarette out the window. "He is."

2

Beneath an oddly gray sky, Rooster walked toward the hulking shadows cast by the enormous warehouse facility at the end of Dover Street. He strode past one alley strewn with garbage, human and otherwise, and then another, the last hope for escape from the dead-end street and the monolithic structures awaiting him. His breath spilled from his nostrils like columns of smoke, partially concealing his face as he pressed on through the cold, hands buried deep in the pockets of his battered leather jacket and chin tucked to chest in an attempt to ward off the occasional bursts of winter wind blowing in off the nearby ocean. Everything was deathly still, and though the constant din of city noises could still be heard, rather than a block or two away, they seemed impossibly far off, as if they were memories of a different city altogether, a deafeningly chaotic city recalled while passing through the mysterious solitude of another.

When he reached the tall chain-link fence surrounding the facility, he noticed the gate was open, a thick padlock and chain dangling free as if left there mistakenly. He hesitated. A nearby security hut beyond was empty, the glass cracked and aged and looking as if it hadn't been cleaned in years. On the far side of the hut, scarred with cracks and occasional tufts of weeds, an enormous parking lot led to a series of loading docks, and amidst the larger warehouses, a smaller building marked OFFICE. Forklifts and other pieces of equipment were scattered about the property as if abandoned long before, and though most of the bays were closed, the few left open revealed enormous but empty storage areas. It looked like some time ago everyone had simply picked up and left.

No one came or went from the office building, and the lone wire-meshed window facing the street was grimy and dark. Had the place gone out of business? He could've sworn he'd passed by here a few days before and it was alive with workers and trucks coming and going, loading and unloading. He tried to remember where he'd heard about the job opportunities here. Had someone told him? Had he seen something at the Unemployment Office? Rooster watched the area a while with the experienced and trained eye of a thief. In time he looked back at the street. It was empty but for bits of trash and debris blowing about in the wind. He checked his watch then gazed at the sky. It normally wasn't so dreary this time of afternoon, but the drab winter sky conspired to cast everything in a dull pall reminiscent of dusk.

After another quick look around, Rooster stepped through the open gate, crossed the parking lot and slipped into the office building.

He found himself in a long, dimly lit corridor that reeked of bleach. With the dull industrial tile floors, low plaster ceilings, steel-encased light fixtures and unimaginative but practical architecture, the building more closely resembled an archaic hospital or dated mental institution than office space.

Rooster pulled off the knit hat he was wearing and held it in his hands. Though the heavy steel entrance door had closed silently behind him he could still see his breath in the hallway. Surely they had heat here, why wouldn't it be on? A small sign protruding from the nearest doorframe read: RECEPTION.

He looked past it to the far end of the corridor, which was draped in darkness. Had something moved just then? Startled, Rooster took a step back. He was certain he'd caught a glimpse of someone shuffling into the cover of darkness, and the sudden sound of labored breath seeping down the hallway in its wake seemed to confirm it. The noise echoed along the walls, transforming into strange, indecipherable whispers.

Whispers that did not sound human.

Rooster stuffed his hat into his back pocket, took a deep breath then ran a hand over his face, eyes trained on the shadows at the end of the hall. *Calm down,* he thought. *It's just the nightmares again.*

An unusual ticking sound drew his attention to the reception office. A lone woman well into her sixties sat behind an inordinately large desk, banging away on an old Olympia typewriter and seemingly oblivious to his presence. A series of metal file cabinets filled out the remaining space behind her. Clad in a dowdy dress and a cardigan sweater thrown over her shoulders for good measure, the receptionist's silver hair was pulled up into a bun, and a pair of half-glasses attached to a chain strung about her neck sat along the bridge of her bulbous nose.

Rooster stepped through the doorway. "Are you still hiring?"

Without looking up from her typewriter the woman retrieved a sheet of paper from a metal bin, slapped it down and slid it over to the edge of the desk. "Fill out this application, front and back. Turn it in to me when you're finished."

Rooster took the form. "Is it always so cold in here?"

"Comes as a shock to most but that's the way it is."

He nodded like he'd understood her answer. "Are you open today?"

"We're always open."

"Then where is everybody?"

The woman's head snapped up, her eyes glaring at him with demonic fury. "Where are *you*?"

Rooster watched the paper fall from his hand as the familiar torment of agonizing screams came to him again. But these were not nightmares or daydreams, he could hear them bellowing from deep within the building, as if people were being tortured in the bowels of the facility. Heart crashing his chest, he backed out into the hallway, terrified. The receptionist's mouth hung open as she panted with anger, spittle dripping from her pale, cracked lips. A quiet growl emanated from her, like the low rumbling snarl of a dog just before it attacks.

He turned and bolted for the front door, slamming into it with his shoulder and stumbling out into the parking lot as it gave way. Staggering forward, he nearly pitched face-first onto the pavement but regained his balance at the last moment and in one frantic, uninterrupted motion, broke into a full run.

He did not look back.

The payphone on the corner was occupied by a rotund woman carrying a brown paper bag filled with groceries. Across the street, Rooster waited, watching from the burned out doorway of an abandoned building only a few blocks from his apartment in the housing projects. Though he couldn't hear what the woman was saying, she was clearly upset and quite animated. He remained huddled in his hiding place until she finally slammed the phone down and stormed from the booth, a look of desperation and confusion creasing her face as she toddled toward the top of the street.

He checked the boulevard in both directions. It was empty. Not even a car or city bus to be found. Moving quickly, he crossed the street, ducked into the phone booth and dug a shred of paper from his jacket pocket. Jotted across it was the information Gaby had written down the last time a call came in. Rooster dropped a dime and punched the numbers.

The connection crackled and hissed but eventually went through and began to ring.

"Hello."

Even after all this time Rooster knew that voice. "Snow."

An exhale of relief and then: "Rooster-man."

He gripped the phone tight and spun around so he could watch the street. "You've been calling me."

"I can't believe it's really you. Didn't know if I'd be able to track you down after all this time."

"Are you here, in the city?"

"Where else would I be?"

"What do you want?"

"We gotta talk."

"I'm not in the life anymore."

"You got no idea what life you're in."

A sharp pain stabbed Rooster's temple. He flinched. "What's that mean?"

"What the hell you think it means? Means I need to talk to you, bro."

"Whatever you're into these days I'm not interested."

"This is serious shit."

"Snow, what do you *want*?"

"I need to see you."

The receptionist's demonic eyes tore through Rooster's memory in strobe-like flashes. "Just leave me alone, man. I got enough problems."

"Motherfucker, I'm trying to help you!"

The visions faded. The fear remained. "Stop calling me."

"You don't hear nothing else I say you better hear this." A crackling hiss bled through the line again. "You need to know what I know."

A burst of wind forced the phone booth door open. He pinned the phone to his shoulder with his ear and sparked a cigarette, making sure to cup the flame until he got it going. "What do you know?"

"I know what you're going through. The headaches, the nightmares. Hearing things, seeing things. Bad things. *Evil* things."

Rooster's eyes watered. He told himself the cold was to blame as a black Crown Vic with a tinted windshield and windows turned at the head of the street and slowly rolled by. *Cop car,* he thought, feeling the muscles in his stomach clench. He hadn't been a criminal in years, but old habits, old fears, died hard. He watched the car until it was out of sight.

"There ain't a lot of time," Snow pressed. "I *need* to see you."

Rooster breathed heavily into the phone in quick nervous bursts. "When?"

"Today."

3

But for their labored breathing, the area is deathly silent. Fog rolls over the open field, cutting across the desolate country road and floating through a thick expanse of forest on the other side. The full moon, still masked by cloud cover, reveals a mist-shrouded landscape of crucified scarecrows, demonic sentries guarding a farmhouse no one would want.

Snow stays in the back of the van with Carbone's body but the rest pile out of the vehicle and wander about the street amidst confusion and high emotions, attempting to gain their bearings while figuring out what to do next.

"What's with all the scarecrows?" Landon asks. "Nothing's grown there for years but weeds, why would they need scarecrows?"

As he surveys the area, Starker still clutches the AK47 he used on the job, his hulking presence and enormous shaved dome daunting even in limited light. He moves to the side of the road. "Maybe it's not crows they're looking to scare off."

"Well if they're meant for me they're working," Nauls says. "Fucking things are creeping me out."

"Yeah Nauls," Landon quips, "they're meant for you. Jesus, what an idiot."

"I'm an idiot? You're the one who stopped here."

"Yeah, because shit-for-brains bit it." Landon jerks a thumb at the van. "And if it's OK with you I've had my fill of smelling dead ass tonight."

Snow emerges from the rear of the van and wipes his bloody hands on his jeans. "What did you say?"

Landon faces him. "You heard me."

"Say it again, motherfucker."

"Hey, I'm sorry Carbone stepped off, but it's nobody's fault but his and you know it. He blew the back doors too early. Total amateur-hour horseshit, he knew better."

"A good man's dead." Snow stepped closer. "Show some respect."

"He fucked up and now we've all got blood on our hands."

"What the hell would you know about it, wheelman*?"*

"Enough to know the stupid bastard could've gotten us all killed. And I didn't hear you making any driver jokes when I was carting your *sorry ass the fuck outta Dodge."*

"You're working my last nerve."

Landon squares his stance. "Blow it out your ass."

Rooster steps between them. "Both of you cool it." He knows he must get the crew focused, split the take and make arrangements to wrap things up one way or another. But it can't be done out in the open, even in a desolate place such as this. One local police car or nosy townsperson passing by is all it'll take to escalate things, and there's been enough escalation tonight. No one was supposed to get hurt. The job had been meticulously planned, rehearsed and timed to the millisecond. Yet there were still mistakes, and what began as a robbery ended in a homicide, one guard dead, two badly injured. And now they've lost one of their own. They have to move and move fast. "We're still on the clock, which means I still call the shots, so get your heads out of your asses and get back in the fucking game. Now."

Snow points at Landon. "We ain't done."

"Any time, douche."

Rooster stands his ground until both men drift away in opposite directions. "All right, let's get inside and finish our business."

Nauls, holding two large canvas duffel bags stuffed with cash, shuffles about like he needs a bathroom. "Can't we find someplace else?"

"I don't like this shit bin any better than you do," Rooster admits, "but it's out of the way and nobody should bother us here. Nauls, you stay with me. Landon, get the van off the street and under cover. Snow,

you and Starker check the place out. It looks deserted but let's be sure."

"OK how come the two brothers got to check the farmhouse out?" Snow cracks. "We more expendable, that it? We ain't special like you white folks."

"Just get it done."

Snow pulls two .45s from the back of his belt and turns to Starker. "All right, big man, let's go."

Apparently mesmerized by the field of rotting scarecrows, Starker does not respond. He stares off into the darkness as if in a trance.

"Come on biggins, time for some recon."

Starker continues to stare at the horrible faces peering across the field through the darkness and fog. Rooster approaches him and cautiously places a hand on his shoulder. "Starker."

He says nothing.

"Stay with me now," Rooster tells him softly. "We need you."

Starker remains locked on the field, one enormous finger resting on the trigger of the AK-47, the other hand sliding almost lovingly back and forth across the top of the weapon in a slow and steady motion. "Something's not right."

"You see something?"

"I feel it. So do you."

He's right, but Rooster can't figure out how Starker knows this. Perhaps he hasn't hidden his anxiety and uneasiness as well as he thought he has. "Maybe we should all go," Rooster suggests. "Check the place out together."

"It doesn't much matter." Starker blinks slowly, his eyes eerily reflecting moonlight. "We're all gonna die tonight."

Memories of Starker's bald head covered in blood flashed before Rooster's eyes, the huge man spitting and slobbering between horrific screams, choking on his own blood and bodily fluids while begging like a child for mercies he would never be granted.

The horrible sounds of that night were the last to leave him, fading gradually like the slowly dying things they were. And like the dead, a gruesome residue remained in their wake. A reminder of their power, perhaps, evidence that such figments of torturous nightmares had, in fact, existed.

Out in the open air the winter wind cut like a razor. Rooster held his ground at the mouth of an alley between a seedy bar and a blown-out storefront, his jacket collar flipped up to protect the back of his neck. A red neon sign advertising the strip joint two doors down blinked with a steady rhythm, painting his face in a strange and frightening haze. His headache had weakened, but a dull pain still lingered behind his eyes. He rubbed his temple and studied the passersby. Everyone on the street seemed suspect, every car a potential menace. He swore he'd seen the same black Crown Vic twice more since he'd walked the eight blocks from the payphone to the agreed upon meeting place, but of course there was no way to know for sure if it was the same vehicle. Even if it was, what would the cops want with him? He'd been doing straight time for years.

He returned his focus to the neighborhood. It was filthy and far from the safest in the city, but Rooster had a good vantage point, as from his position he could clearly see people approaching from either direction. Though like the rest of the city many of the buildings sat vacant and rotting, this was predominantly a commercial area that still crackled with intensity and life. Heavy traffic clogged both lanes, filling the air with a glut of sickening exhaust fumes, and numerous souls of varied descriptions hurried along the sidewalks, several scowling at him as if he'd done something to personally offend them but most with their heads bowed and eyes averted. At the end of the block an old homeless man collapsed on the sidewalk and lay still. After watching him a moment Rooster realized the man's breath was no longer forming clouds in the cold air. Perhaps he'd died. No one seemed to care.

It was then that Rooster noticed a bald man of perhaps sixty standing across the street watching him, features unremarkable but for a pair of piercing ice-blue eyes. Dressed entirely in black—suit, shoes and overcoat—it wasn't until the man glided a bit further down the block that Rooster saw the white collar and realized he was looking at a priest. The closer the man got the more disheveled he became, his clothes wrinkled and soiled and his face creased with age and looking as if it needed a good scrubbing.

Ignoring the traffic, the priest recklessly crossed the street, eyes locked on Rooster even after several drivers hit their horns and one car nearly struck him. While still several feet away, the priest raised a hand and pointed at him. "You, I—I know you!" he called. "I *know* you!"

Rooster shook his head and waved the man off, though oddly enough, the closer the priest got the more familiar he became. He couldn't quite place him but was convinced he knew him from somewhere.

Just as the priest made it to the sidewalk, another man appeared out of the crowd and cut him off, blocking his path.

The afro gave him away. Snow, looking like he always had, dressed in jeans, sneakers and an old army jacket thrown over a sweatshirt, extended a hand, holding it up between himself and the priest as their eyes met. Neither moved; two statues in a sea of humanity.

Rooster stepped out of the alley, approached them. The priest looked over Snow's shoulder, enraged.

"I *know* you!"

"Keep moving, padre," Snow said evenly. "I ain't playing with you. *Move.*"

Defeated, the priest slipped away, looking back every few seconds until he'd been completely absorbed by the crowd, carried off down the street with the rest.

Rooster started after him but Snow grabbed his arm, firmly enough to stop him but with enough restraint to let him know the move wasn't a challenge.

"Let him go, man."

"He's right, I—we know each other, I—"

"Just let him go." When Rooster relaxed Snow released him. "You don't look no different."

They shook hands. Snow's palm was cold, rough and covered in calluses. "Neither do you," Rooster sighed. "But we are different, aren't we?"

Nearby, overhead trains rumbled along rusted tracks. The noise seemed to distract Snow for a moment. "Let's get off the street." He motioned to the bar behind them. "Catch some heat."

The bar was dark, with scarred linoleum floors, low ceilings and only two small windows on the front wall. A scattering of tables and chairs filled the area, while a row of dark booths lined one wall and a bar filled the back. A jukebox kitty-cornered nearby sat quietly. The bartender, an overweight guy with a shock of unruly salt-and-pepper hair, chatted quietly with what was probably a regular, both staring at a small television suspended in the corner showing an old black-and-white horror movie. Otherwise the place was empty.

Rooster and Snow ordered a couple beers then took them over to the booth farthest from the bar and sat down.

"It's good to see you, man." Snow slowly caressed his beer bottle, focusing on it rather than Rooster. "Just sucks it has to be like this."

After a long swallow of beer Rooster slid a black plastic ashtray from the corner of the table into the center and lit a cigarette. "What's going on, Snow?"

He was about to answer when a bloodcurdling scream exploded through the bar.

Rooster reached to his belt for a gun that wasn't there, a gun that hadn't been there in years. Snow cocked his head in the direction of the television, where a ghoul was staggering through a cemetery shrouded in mist, closing in on a buxom young maiden with the ability to scream at octaves capable of shattering glass.

"Jesus H." He rubbed his temples. "Could've lived without that."

"Never seen you so jumpy, Rooster-man. You were always cold as ice."

"The priest, who was he?"

"I don't know."

"He knew me. And I knew him. I just can't remember how."

"You'll figure it out."

"Can't figure out much of anything lately. The strangest shit's happening. I can't make sense of any of it." He took a deep drag on his cigarette, blew out a cloud of smoke and watched it climb toward the ceiling. "Look, I—"

"Feels like you went to sleep and woke up in the middle of your life," Snow interrupted, voice unusually quiet, "and now you can't remember how the hell you got here."

Rooster stabbed the cigarette between his lips and left it there so he could put his hands flat on the table between them and better conceal the fact that they were shaking. He nodded. "What's happening to us?"

Up close Snow's eyes were bloodshot and heavy, like he'd been crying recently, hadn't slept in a while, or both. He smelled vaguely of cheap aftershave. "What do you know about demons?"

"*Demons*? You mean like—"

"Like all kinds of crazy shit runs through your head, then you start hearing things. Screams mostly, or whispers that don't make no sense. And just when you think it can't get no worse, you start seeing shit. Not people, not…not exactly. But they look like people…least until they don't."

The receptionist, Rooster thought, shrugging off a chill. "I don't believe in demons."

"Yeah neither do I but they don't seem to give a shit." Snow downed some beer then let out a quiet belch under his breath and looked to the door as if expecting someone to burst through it at any moment. "Not too long ago I got some information." He leaned closer, across the table. "And ever since then these other motherfuckers have been following me. Never up close, always a ways back, watching from their cars, Crown Vics—big black bastards—that's what they drive."

"Cops?"

"These ain't cops."

"Who are they?"

"They been following me for weeks. After today they'll be following you."

"Why?" With manic repetition Rooster puffed his cigarette. "What do they want?"

"You remember the night Carbone died?"

Rooster began to perspire as flashes of farmhouse, blood and scarecrows filled his memory. "Some."

No longer able to contain his nervousness, Snow abruptly stood up and made a beeline for the jukebox. He dropped a coin in, made a selection then gave the bartender and his friend a long look that said: *This is going to make hearing the television more difficult but let's not make a big deal about it or you'll force me to do some really unpleasant shit to you.* Both men looked away without comment and Snow slowly strode back to the booth as The Police's *Spirits in the Material World* kicked in.

"You said I needed to know what you know."

Rooster crushed his cigarette in the ashtray. "So tell me."

"What do you remember about the night Carbone died?"

"Come on, man, what the hell's going on?"

"Do it."

"The armored car robbery, the last job we pulled as a crew," he said. "Everything went according to plan until Carbone fucked up and blew the back doors too early. The third guard was waiting on him. Carbone took a shotgun blast dead in the gut. Starker wasted the guard, shot him in the face, killed him instantly." He remembered the young man's head as it exploded, a crimson mist of blood, brains and skull spraying everything, and all of them. "You got Carbone back to the van while Nauls and I handled the other two guards and took care of the swag. Landon was the wheelman. We got out ahead of the cops, ended up in the middle of nowhere at some deserted old farmhouse. Carbone died in the van."

Snow nodded. "Then what?"

"You were there."

"Pretend I wasn't."

Rooster fidgeted in his seat. It felt like thousands of insects were scurrying over every inch of his body. He scratched at his head and suddenly found himself checking the door every few seconds as well. "I don't..."

"You don't know."

Shadows along the ceiling shifted, elongated.

"We split the take," he finally said. "Then we took off."

"That how you remember it?"

"I think so but I can't..." Rooster took another swig of beer. "I can't remember exactly, it...the whole thing seems like a dream."

"I couldn't remember nothing either."

The man at the bar, a middle-aged guy wearing some sort of workman's uniform, hopped down from his stool and slipped through a nearby door marked RESTROOMS.

"The more I thought about it," Snow continued, "the worse it got. I couldn't remember the rest of that night no matter how hard I tried. It was like it was just...*gone*. All I knew was whatever happened scared the shit out of me, made me scared like I never even knew I could be. I'm talking about the kind of fear you feel right down to your nuts, man. The kind that makes you shit in your pants like a baby sliding out lunch. You know what I mean."

Rooster did know. He swallowed so hard he gagged.

"Like you, I thought I was losing my goddamn mind." Snow sat back with an air of defiance. "It's like there was something right on my ass, something evil. I couldn't take no more. I stopped sleeping, stopped eating, just locked myself up in my apartment and hid out. I wanted to kill myself but I was afraid of the other side. Ain't exactly lived the life of a saint, right?"

The bartender was staring at them intently. When he realized Rooster had caught him he quickly looked away and busied himself.

"That's when that woman started hanging outside my apartment wanting to talk to me all the time." His face twisted. "I didn't know who she was, didn't know what I'd done. I don't even remember it. I was on H when it went down and was hurting so bad for a fix I was out of my mind. I never meant to hurt her."

"I never knew you did heroin."

Snow sighed helplessly. "Neither did I."

"You're not making any sense. What the hell are you talking about?"

"I tried to do straight time, man, for real. I tried."

"I believe you."

"I got a janitor gig at this office building a few blocks from my crib. I was going crazy but I showed up on time every night, did my thing and minded my own business, played by the rules, closed my eyes to the demons and the screams and that woman always staring at me. I'd walk there, work the overnight shift then walk home in the morning. I'm there about a week when I notice this old dude following me one night. Skinny little white cat with glasses. Real Poindexter-looking motherfucker. At first I think maybe he's a cop, but he don't look like no cop I ever seen, looks more like a professor or some shit. He shows up every night, tails me from my apartment to work, and then he's gone. So one night I get a lead on him, take a corner and duck into a doorway. He comes by and I grab his narrow ass." Snow ran a hand over his face. He too had begun to perspire. "I'm about to rack me some old white man when he starts talking about that night at the farmhouse, all the shit I'm going through and how he can help me. Motherfucker knew more about me than I did, man. Said he had answers, said he knew what happened to us that night. He said it was time we knew the truth. And that's exactly what he laid on me. Only now sometimes I wish he didn't. Sometimes not knowing was better." He bowed his head in an attempt to mask the tears filling his eyes. "Ain't that a bitch? We never had a goddamn chance, man, none of us."

"Who was this guy?"

"What they done to us wasn't right, Rooster, it wasn't right. We did some bad shit but we're human beings, man, we fucking *human beings*."

"What who did to us? What are you saying?"

Snow reached into his jacket, put something on the table and slid it over to him. When he pulled his hand away a small key was revealed. "Opens a locker at the bus station downtown," he said. "Take it. Use it."

Rooster nonchalantly covered it with his palm. "What am I gonna find?"

"Everything I know. Everything you need to know. All the proof I got from Poindexter." He checked the door once, then again just a second or two later. "They're after me, man, and they know I'm trying to pass the information to you. Once they know you got it, they're gonna come after you, too."

"Why are you giving this to me, why not one of the others?"

Snow shrugged. "Carbone's dead. Nauls is a retard. Landon's an asshole, and Starker—shit—that boy's stone psycho. Whatever

Hell them motherfuckers are burning in they deserve."

"I'm not so sure anybody deserves to burn in Hell."

"Makes sense if you're the one burning."

Rooster slid the key to the edge of the table then pocketed it. "You know where any of them are?"

"Last I heard Nauls and Landon were still in the city and still in the life. Starker supposedly caught his old lady banging some guy. Put a .38 in her pussy and pulled the trigger, then he beat the dude into a coma, ripped his junk off and stuffed it so far up his ass they had to do surgery to get the shit out. Couple days later they both died. Starker got away. Word was he headed down to Mexico or some shit."

"They ever catch him?"

"Don't know." He wiped the tears from his eyes then killed his beer. "Don't care."

"What happened to us that night, Snow?"

"Go open that locker."

"Why don't you just tell me?"

Snow smiled, but it was the smile of the damned. "You wouldn't believe me even if I did."

"Try me."

"You got to see for yourself."

Across the barroom, the restroom door opened with a scraping sound and Rooster saw the same man exit, wander back to the bar and return to the stool he'd vacated moments before. As the door slowly swung shut, he saw a moist and filthy tile floor littered with scraps of toilet paper and trash, and something else moving along the wet tiles toward the toilet stalls on the back wall of the bathroom. Like the severed appendage from some scale-covered creature, it slithered about in a snakelike motion, revealing a pale tentacle several inches thick and at least three feet long. Rooster sat up straighter, squinting through the shadows in an attempt to bring the thing into focus, but the door had closed. He glanced at Snow, who hadn't seen it but looked as if he had. Rooster turned away, hopeful he might be able to obliterate what he'd just seen and knew to be impossible, but when he returned his gaze to the bar he saw the man grinning at him with malicious glee. Both he and the bartender began to laugh.

Rooster shuddered. "We need to get outta here."

"Don't matter for me no more."

Rooster reached across the table, took hold of Snow's wrist. It was cold as ice. He let go. "I'm not leaving you here, man."

"I'm already dead. Been dead and buried for years." Snow's eyes suddenly looked empty, even more hopeless than before. "And so have you."

4

He'd stood in the bus terminal for more than an hour. There was no sign of the Crown Vic or anyone following him on foot, but Rooster couldn't shake the feeling he'd been tailed. So he stayed put, watched and waited.

People came and went, maintenance workers and ticket agents busied themselves with various duties, an occasional policeman drifted through, and a handful of homeless people sat in corners or, like many of the waiting passengers, occupied one of the numerous plastic chairs bolted to the floor in clusters and rows throughout the station.

The entire place smelled like a combination of filthy socks, urine and body odor, all of it made more oppressive by smothering bursts of forced hot air from an archaic heating system set far too high.

Directly across from the wall Rooster was leaned against stood a bank of lockers. He'd been fingering the key in his pocket since he arrived, and though he'd yet to approach it, he'd already zeroed in on the appropriate locker. He still couldn't be certain he wanted to know what was waiting for him behind that little metal door. His life was complicated and confused enough. Did he really need to up the ante? Then again, could he afford not to? Snow had assured him the answers to his torment could be found within and he had no reason to doubt him. Even if it was a Pandora's Box (and Rooster was certain it would be), how could he *not* open it?

Fuck it.

Pushing away from the wall, Rooster walked toward the lockers, casually sliding his hand from his pocket and holding the key down by his thigh.

They're after me, man.

No one seemed to notice as he closed on the locker, pushed the key into the slot then pulled the latch.

And they know I'm trying to pass the information to you.

Rooster swung open the door, saw a black leather briefcase inside.

Once they know you got it, they're gonna come after you, too.

Heart racing, he reached inside, yanked it free and walked away, leaving the locker open and the key still in the lock.

Moving through the sliding front doors and into the cold but fresh air, Rooster hurried down the block and slipped into the first alley he came to, using it to cut through to the next busy street, where he disappeared into the flow of the crowd on the nearest sidewalk.

Night fell across the city as darkness swept through him, awakening demons eager to tear at a soul already in ruin.

The fires of Hell burned on.

He'd always felt relatively safe at the apartment. Now he wasn't so sure. As he'd crossed town he noticed no tails, but knew he was being watched. Even when he'd hurried across the courtyard and into the projects, the area cold and empty but for one lone child sitting on a stoop a few buildings down, he still felt an overwhelming sense that someone was following him. Once inside he bolted the apartment door, pulled the shades on the windows then set the briefcase on the kitchen table. He remained still and quiet a moment, listening. Some distant sounds from neighboring units bled through the thin walls and the building settled and creaked against the increasing wind, but he could discern nothing out of the ordinary. Next he returned to the windows facing the street and courtyard, spending a few seconds at each one, pulling back the shades enough to peek out and inspect the area for intruders, strange cars or individuals. Nothing.

Rooster checked his watch. Gaby wouldn't get home from work for about another hour. He'd have the place to himself for a while. With only a small hanging light in the kitchen illuminating the area, he grabbed a bottle of whiskey from the cupboard and poured a shot. As the booze burned then warmed him, he pulled up a chair and sat at the table, eyeing the briefcase as if he expected it to do something other than sit there like the inanimate object it was. A basic black leather model, it had only one main zippered compartment and no markings or personalized indications of any kind. He looked at his hands. Still shaking. *For Christ's sake,* he thought. *Get a grip.* Back in the day he'd been known for his remarkable cool in the face of danger. Hadn't he? Like so much else it was lost in a dark sea of partial memories, fractured dreams and uncertain yesterdays.

He pounded down another mouthful of whiskey then held the empty shot glass out before him until he'd willed the trembling to stop. Hand finally steady, or at least reasonably close, he put the glass aside, unzipped the briefcase and reached inside. His hand returned holding a large manila folder held shut by two thick rubber bands. The only other item in the briefcase was a hardcover book. Rooster placed both on the table before him, quickly inspected the briefcase to make certain he'd gotten everything then put it on the floor by his feet.

There were no markings on the exterior of the manila folder itself but it was stuffed with various documents. The book was black, had no dust-jacket and was badly worn, the back cover blank. Rooster flipped it over.

A bright red inverted pentagram filled the front cover, the title in matching color above it: *DEMONOLOGY: Incantations.*

He vaulted back and away from the table as if hit with an electrical charge, eyes transfixed on the pentagram as his chair tipped over backwards and fell to the floor.

What do you know about demons?

Fear crashed him like a wave, surging up through his legs, guts, and into his chest, chills firing through his shoulders and neck, his eyes burning as the uncontrollable shivers returned, this time violently throttling his entire body.

I'm so cold…

Voices in his head…familiar voices…

I'm so…so…cold…

Flashes of a face stricken with horror, mouth ripped open

into a bloody and devilish grin, the skin on the cheeks and forehead moving and tenting impossibly, like something was trapped beneath and trying to get out, something barbed and small slithering for purchase…

Help me…God in Heaven, help me!

Clutching his temples, Rooster staggered back, muttering prayers he hadn't recited since childhood.

Shadowy visions of a man standing over a body, the stomach cavity split open, his hands grasping a tangle of viscera—ropes of blood and guts squished between his fingers—laughing and squatting closer to the carnage, his face spattered with blood and colorless jellylike fluids, shards of human flesh dangling from the corners of his mouth…and all the while, horrible screams of agony bellowed amidst vicious laughter…

It wasn't until Rooster felt the far kitchen wall against his back and slid down to the floor in a heap, sobbing and moaning like a traumatized child, that the visions and voices finally retreated.

But not before he realized that the face of the man he'd seen—the man in the shadows disemboweling another human being—was his own.

5

They move across the field in a staggered line, weapons drawn, the overgrown grass and weeds nearly to their waists. The fog moves with them as they negotiate the uneven terrain, slowly, cautiously, the darkness deepening with each step they take. The scarecrows watch from their wooden crosses, some nailed, some tied with rotting lengths of rope, manlike ghouls in old and torn denim overalls and decayed work shirts, hands of straw protruding from the sleeves like talons, legs dangling, vanishing into the tall grass. With badly worn, stuffed and filthy burlap sacks for heads, their mouths are stiff grim lines of worn leather thread sewn into the fabric in a disturbing crisscross pattern, their eyes sunken black holes, as if the sockets have been long-since picked clean.

Starker is in the lead. He stops and the others follow suit. His eyes pan the area, take in each scarecrow. No one speaks for several seconds. The night is unnaturally quiet. "Come on, what is this bullshit?" Landon moans. "We're in the middle of nowhere. Nobody's been here in years. Why bother with the house at all? Let's split the take now. What difference does it make?"

"We are pretty far from the road." Nauls looks back. "Haven't seen any cars pass by the whole time we've been here."

Ignoring them, Rooster looks to Starker. "What's wrong?"

"Notice anything about those scarecrows?"

"I'm trying not to notice them at all," Nauls says.

Landon rolls his eyes. "What are you, five-fucking-years-old? There's nobody here but us, let's get on with it."

"Starker," Rooster presses, "what is it?"

"There are six of them," he says, "six scarecrows." Snow shrugs. "So?"

"There are six of us."

Rooster studied the shadows cast throughout the kitchen, opaque swathes of darkness slashing the light. Still on the floor and covered in a thin sheen of perspiration, his flesh was clammy and hot but his breathing and heartbeat had finally returned to normal. He wasn't sure why the pentagram specifically had triggered such terror, he only knew it had. His fear had weakened, though it was still close by, and a steady throb above his eyes signaled another headache was on its way. Luckily the pain hadn't kicked in yet.

With a willful grunt he forced himself to his feet, and on shaky legs, returned to the table. Once he'd righted the chair he dropped back into it then cautiously reached for the book. The cover was old and shabby, rough in his hands. Without looking at the pentagram, he quickly flipped open the cover.

In rather ornate script, printed on the first page:

"The other shape,

If shape it might be call'd, that shape had none, Distinguishable in member, joint, or limb;

Or substance might be call'd that shadow seem'd; For each seem'd either; black it stood as night, Fierce as ten furies, terrible as Hell,

And shook a dreadful dart; what seem'd his head The likeness of a kingly crown had on.

Satan was now at hand; and from his seat The monster, moving onward, came as fast

With horrid strides; Hell trembled as he strode."

—John Milton

The pages of the book looked even older than the cover. Made of stiff thick parchment, faded and badly furrowed, they mostly sported what appeared to be very old drawings of demons. Hideous winged creatures with leering eyes, many with horns and cloven hooves, huddled in darkness. Others perched over the beds of unsuspecting sleeping victims or sat on blasphemous thrones of human bone. Others still were illustrated engulfed in flames or in mid-flight amidst the clouds, tangled in battle with angels. But for the cover and Milton quote, the text was written in Latin, in a calligraphy-like style, as if scribed by some mad medieval monk in the bowels of a candlelit monastery. Just touching the book made Rooster uncomfortable, so he quickly flipped through the remaining pages of lurid illustrations and indecipherable text then slammed it shut. Placing it facedown, he took another shot of whiskey.

When his nerves had settled a bit, he turned his attention to the manila folder. Six files were individually bound and stacked within, the front of each marked with a name: *Paul Carbone, Terrell Snow, Anthony Starker, Perry Nauls, Thomas Landon,* and the sixth and final file, his own, *Michael Cantrell.*

Rather than immediately delve into his own file, he decided to begin with someone else's. *Carbone's dead,* he reasoned, *I'll start there.* He opened the file to find a mug-shot staring back at him. He hadn't seen Carbone in anything but nightmares for years, and looking into the man's eyes now shook him to the core. He remembered Carbone as a short and stocky man of few words, with a dry but cutting sense of humor and a laid-back personality. But mostly he remembered him screaming in agony and begging for his mother as he bled to death.

Rooster moved to the next page. All of Carbone's stats were there: his full legal name, date of birth and social security number. Lower on the page it listed no living next-of-kin, the fact that he'd never graduated high school and had no formal education beyond the tenth grade, and that he was unmarried and had no children. The next page revealed a bullet list regarding his criminal record, which went back to his late teens and covered everything from petty theft to numerous sexual assaults and indecent exposures, to child pornography charges to assault and battery. The final entry, highlighted in yellow, documented his final arrest and conviction, the rape and stabbing death of a seven-year-old girl. He'd received two Life Sentences with no chance of parole, and according to the entry, had been serving them at the time this information had been originally compiled.

"That's bullshit," Rooster muttered. He hadn't known Carbone that well, but Snow had, and he'd have never aligned himself with that kind of scum. Carbone was a criminal like the rest of them for sure, but he wasn't a sexual deviant or a child killer. They were thieves, they didn't rape and butcher children. And besides, even if Carbone *had* been guilty of such things and given those sentences, why hadn't he been inside serving them? Had they let him out? Had he escaped? None of it made any sense.

He went back to the photograph. It wasn't an actual mug-shot, as he'd originally thought, it only looked like one. Instead it was simply a headshot of Carbone from the neck up, a black background behind him and his name stenciled along the bottom white border.

The last page of Carbone's file contained a single word: DECEASED.

The file seemed thrown together and incomplete, as if someone had hastily transcribed a few important basic points, added a photograph then bound and stuffed the information into a folder. Rooster put it aside and moved to the next one.

Starker's file contained a similar photograph and described him as a former Army Ranger that had received a dishonorable discharge and had served four years in a military prison for assaulting an officer. His personal stats were listed as well, including that he was single and had no children. His civilian criminal record began after his stint in the service, and consisted mostly of assaults and illegal weapons charges. It also listed him as a member of a radical political and paramilitary group the government had labeled as a terrorist organization responsible for the numerous bombings of several government buildings. His final conviction described him as one of a three-man team that had firebombed the campaign office of a political candidate their organization opposed. Four people had been killed in the bombing, including two women, one of them eight-months pregnant. Starker, along with his accomplices, had received Death.

This information was more believable—Starker had always been the most violent of the crew and the most unpredictable—but again, much of it made no sense. Starker wasn't single, he was married—or at least had been, according to Snow he'd since murdered his wife—and although Rooster did know about Starker's prior military service, he knew nothing about this radical political organization he'd supposedly been a member of, and certainly nothing of the firebombing of a campaign office. And again, if that were true, and he'd received a death sentence and had already begun to serve time on Death Row as the information suggested, how had he been with them the night of the armored car job?

"He couldn't be."

This time the final page contained the word TERMINATED.

Rooster reached for the bottle, poured another shot of whiskey.

Terminated? But Starker wasn't dead. Unless they'd killed him…whoever the hell *they* were.

Next came Nauls. The face in the photograph showed that same narrow face with the beady eyes he remembered. A closely-cropped beard and wild nest of curly hair coupled with his thin build gave him the look of a stoner or wannabe rock musician, and in reality, he'd been a little of both. In fact it was strange to see his eyes at all, as Nauls had almost always worn a pair of dark sunglasses, the lenses small, round and tight to his face. His file described a man who had been in and out of jail from the time he'd been a teenager, and who began serving prison time at only twenty. Predominantly a thief, he'd been arrested countless times for B&Es, purse-snatching, shoplifting, and drug possession. By all accounts Nauls had been a petty thief but not the least bit violent. In his mid-twenties he'd graduated to bank robbery and done time for it in federal prison. Like so many others, Nauls had come out of prison far worse than he'd gone in, as according to the paperwork, two months after his release he was arrested for another bank robbery, one that ended particularly violently.

The report claimed Nauls, cornered in the bank, had taken several tellers and the bank manager hostage. After a fourteen-hour standoff, Nauls had been refused the helicopter he'd demanded for his escape, and as a result had executed a female teller and then the bank manager. He was shot by a SWAT sniper moments later. Hit in the upper right chest, Nauls survived.

Ironically, he was sentenced to Death.

Rooster knew Nauls to be the most harmless member of the crew, and also the least violent. He spent most of his time smoking pot, chasing women, strumming an old guitar he loved and watching cartoons. He was a thief—and a good one—but not that bright and generally clueless. He was damaged, the kind of guy who had done hard time and wasn't really cut out for it. Far as he knew, Nauls had an extensive criminal past but he wasn't a killer, and the idea that he could've executed two people in cold blood seemed beyond belief.

The last page was the same as Starker's. TERMINATED.

Landon too looked exactly how Rooster remembered him, as a man of average build with short dark hair receded to the middle of his scalp, hazel eyes, a permanent five o'clock shadow, an aquiline nose with flared nostrils and a mouth that seemed perpetually set in a wiseass smirk. His file depicted a man with a long criminal record, the majority of his arrests involving car theft or driving violations. Landon had always been a car nut, and was one of the best drivers Rooster had ever seen—certainly the best he'd ever worked with—and though he had a temper, complained endlessly and never backed down from a physical confrontation, he'd never been a particularly violent individual. He had the ability to be violent, and Rooster remembered more than one occasion when Landon had handled himself competently in physical skirmishes, but for the most part it was his mouth one had to look out for. Landon could cut someone to shreds verbally without even trying. He'd begun his criminal career stealing cars as a teenager, and by the time he was in his twenties he'd done time for auto theft and for two counts of aggravated assault. In and out of prison for most of his twenties, he was later arrested as the wheelman on a jewelry store heist. He and his accomplices had escaped but not before police were on them, and in the resulting high-speed chase Landon plowed directly through a police barricade, killing two police officers. After losing control of the car he struck a group of pedestrians, killing two—including an elderly man and a woman who had been holding her four-year-old child at the time—and seriously injuring several others. Landon drove on. Several blocks later his tires were shot out and he crashed into a telephone pole. One of his accomplices died in the crash. The other survived but was gunned down as he attempted to flee the scene. Landon suffered several minor injuries but survived. He was given Life without parole.

Same final page: TERMINATED.

Rooster shook his head in disbelief and turned to Snow's file.

Terrell Snow looked the same in the photo as he had at the bar earlier. His record was long and varied, consisting of everything from theft to assault to attempted murder to drug charges. A lifelong criminal and former gang member, Snow had, according to the paperwork at least, struggled with heroin addiction at one point earlier in his life. Something even Snow himself had been unaware of.

Which means it's crap, Rooster thought.

After a long criminal career, the result of which was Snow spending the majority of his adult life in prison, he'd been convicted of beating a young woman to death in her apartment during a botched robbery.

I didn't know who she was, didn't know what I'd done. The crime was listed as 'particularly vicious' in that the woman had apparently not resisted her assailant but had been beaten so mercilessly that police were initially unable to determine if the victim was male or female.

I don't even remember it. I was on H when it went down and was hurting so bad for a fix I was out of my mind.

Snow received Life without parole.

I never meant to hurt her. Last page: TERMINATED.

I'm already dead. Been dead and buried for years.

Of course he'd meant it figuratively, but Rooster couldn't help but wonder if there wasn't more truth to Snow's statement than he'd originally been willing to give it. He put the file aside and eyed the final one, his own. He downed another shot, felt his head swim a bit.

There he was looking back at himself in a photograph Rooster had no memory of ever posing for. His basic stats were all correct, as were the entries concerning his criminal record.

He'd served several jail sentences over the years, having been arrested numerous times for theft and assault (once with a deadly weapon), but he'd only gone to prison twice. Once for his involvement in an armed bank robbery for which he served six years of a ten-year sentence, and the other, his final conviction for which he received Death.

This is ridiculous, he thought. *How could I have served time on Death Row without having any memory of it? And what am I doing out even if I did?*

He continued reading. He'd been given Death for the torture and murder of a man named Roland McKay.

A Roman Catholic priest.

Rooster's breath caught at the base of his throat, and he brought a hand to his mouth for fear a literal gasp might escape his lips. His mind replayed the memory of the priest accosting him on the street. How could this be? He had no memory of ever murdering anyone, much less a priest. He was a thief like the rest of the crew, not some sadistic psychopath. And if he'd killed this man, how could he be stalking the city streets pointing an accusatory finger at anyone?

The files were all there in front of him in black and white. But not one of them made any goddamn sense. The information couldn't be true.

Hesitantly, Rooster turned to the final page of his file.

TERMINATED.

6

He gathered up the files and threw them back into the briefcase on the floor. As he reached for the book he saw a business card lying on the table he hadn't noticed previously. An address had been written on one side, a phone number on the other. Both had been written in ballpoint pen, and though legible, appeared hastily scribbled by a less than steady hand. Mind still reeling, Rooster considered the card a moment then grabbed the wall phone and dialed.

"We're sorry," a recorded female voice replied, "the number you dialed is not in service. Please check the number and try again."

He hung up and tried again. Perhaps the five shots of Jack Daniels had caused him to misdial. This time he concentrated on each number to make sure he got it right, but the same recording answered. He slammed the phone down, fear and uncertainty giving way to anger. It was short-lived. Within seconds of hanging up, the phone began to ring. Startled, he slowly reached for the receiver and brought it to his ear. He could hear breathing. "Yes?"

"Hello, Mr. Cantrell." The voice was raspy and weak, like it belonged to a very tired old man. "You dialed the number. Obviously you've seen the files."

"Who are you?"

"Look on the other side of the card," the voice instructed. "Do you see an address there?"

"Yes."

"Be there tomorrow morning. Ten o'clock."

"No," Rooster said, "let's do this tonight. I want this over with."

"Tomorrow morning. Ten o'clock."

"How will I know you?"

"I'll know you. Come alone."

The line clicked, died and was replaced with a dial tone. Rooster grabbed the card, read the address again. It meant nothing to him, just an address. His mind on overload, he tried to consider the information in the files again but couldn't make sense of it. He knew those men. None of them were guilty of such things. And why in God's name would he have tortured and murdered anyone? Why would someone invent pasts and former crimes for him and the others? Why would they compile files with false information about things that never happened? What could possibly be the point?

Rooster snatched the phone up again and this time dialed the number Snow had given him. He'd promised the information would answer his questions and tell him everything he needed to know. It hadn't. The line rang several times without reply, and he was just about to hang up when he heard a soft click. The ringing ceased. "Hello?" he said a moment later.

"Who is this?" The voice was strange. Though male, it had a synthetic quality to it, like the person was speaking through a machine of some sort.

"Where's Snow?"

"Who is this?"

"I need to speak to Snow, put him on the phone."

"Who *is* this?"

"Who the hell is *this*?"

The voice answered in what began as English but quickly morphed into an indecipherable tongue, eventually becoming a deafening screech somewhere between a scream and a rage-filled, animal-like howl. Rooster pulled the phone from his ear, holding it several inches away, but the horrible wailing continued. He knew those sounds. He'd heard them before, somewhere in a distant and blurred past. Wracked with another wave of terror, he hung the phone up and backed away, stumbling into the kitchen table as he went.

A loud clap behind him sent a shiver through his body as he spun in the direction of the noise.

He'd knocked the book to the floor.

He retrieved it, tossed it on the table then grabbed the whiskey and poured another shot.

The violent tremor in his hands had returned.

The jangle of Gaby's keys in the lock startled him. Huddled at the kitchen table, Rooster had become so enthralled while further studying the book on Demonology that he hadn't heard Gaby ascending the stairs to their apartment. He'd stopped at a depiction of a particularly gruesome-looking demon with blackened wings and a hideous, half-goat, half-human face. Squatting atop a mountain of mangled and dismembered human bodies, in one of its clawed hands it held the severed head of a woman, and in the other what appeared to be a male member. Rooster rubbed his eyes, looked over at Gaby.

"Hey," she said, closing the door behind her. In her arms she held a brown paper bag from the neighborhood grocer. Beneath her heavy winter coat she wore a plain dress and a pair of black heels. Her hair was up and held in place with a clip but had become mussed, probably from the wind. She looked tired. "How'd the job hunt go?"

"Lock the door."

She did, then put the bag on the counter, removed her coat and walked over to the table. They kissed. "You OK? Why is it so dark in here?" She headed for a lamp in the den.

"Don't."

Gaby stopped, looked at him quizzically.

"Just don't. OK?"

As if not entirely sure what to make of him, she moved back toward the table. "What's that?" she asked, referring to the book. Before he could answer she saw the illustration. "What are you doing with that?"

Rooster closed the book so she could see the cover.

"Demonology? I don't want that in the house."

"Neither do I," he sighed.

"Then get rid of it." She picked up the whiskey bottle and took it with her to the counter, where she dropped it off then began emptying the grocery bag. "Sorry babe, I had a long day, just didn't feel like cooking." She held up two TV dinners. "Got you that Salisbury steak one you like, OK?"

He followed her to the counter, grabbed his cigarettes and lit one. "Do you believe in them?"

"Demons?" she asked, busying herself with the oven. "Do you?"

"The book supposedly shows what they look like, and it has incantations written in Latin. Is that how people summon them?"

"Why would anyone want to summon demons?" Gaby unwrapped both dinners and left them on top of the stove. "It'll just take a minute to preheat and I'll get these in."

"I called Snow," he said. "We met this afternoon."

"Is that where you got the book?"

"That and the briefcase," he said, motioning to it.

"Why would he give you a book like that? And what's in the briefcase?"

Rooster took a couple drags before answering. "It's better if you don't know."

"Is that why he kept calling? So he could tell you secrets?"

"Gaby," he said, clearing his throat. "I need to ask you something."

She stopped futzing about the kitchen and focused on him, dark eyes narrowed as if trying to see him more clearly. "OK."

"How long have we known each other?"

"Seems like forever, doesn't it?"

"How did we meet?" he asked.

She smiled uncomfortably. "Are you serious?"

"Yes."

"You don't remember?"

Tears filled his eyes. He shook his head no, brought the cigarette to his lips and drew on it, hard. "I can't…I don't know what's happening to me but—something's wrong, Gaby—I think I'm losing my mind or…worse."

She put a hand on his forehead. "You're warm. Feels like you're running a bit of a temp. Let me get you some aspirin."

He gently pulled her hand away but held on tight, watching her blur through his tears. "I know I know you but…Gaby…I don't know who you are. I'm not even sure who I am."

"You haven't slept, you're drinking, and now you've got a bad influence from your past giving you scary books and making things worse." She moved by him, grabbed the book from the table and tucked it into the briefcase. "No wonder you're not feeling well and can't think clearly. Get this out of here or I'll take it out to the Dumpster myself. I'm serious."

"I need you to tell me, Gaby, please, I—"

"You need something to eat, a nice hot shower and some sleep. I'll—"

"Stop it!" He smashed a fist on the counter. The entire room shook. "Fucking answer me!"

Gaby remained where she was, hugging herself.

In a tiny voice she said, "You're frightening me."

"I'm sorry." Rooster threw the remains of his cigarette into the kitchen sink then began pacing like a caged animal. "I'm sorry, I—Jesus *Christ*, what's happening to me?"

She cautiously stepped closer. "It's going to be all right."

No longer able to control it, he wept openly.

Closing the gap between them, Gaby cupped his face in her hands. "Look at me." He did. *"It's going to be all right."*

"Am I crazy?"

She pulled him into her, held his head tight to her breasts and kissed the top of his head. "No, baby, you're not crazy. You're just trying to find your way."

"I think they're after me, Gaby, I think the demons are—something's happened, I can't remember things and—"

"Nothing can hurt you while you're with me." She gave him a quick wink. "My love's *way* too powerful for any demon, real or imagined. They mess with my man I'll kick the slithery-tailed little pukes back to Hell where they belong."

Rooster wanted to smile, but the terror remained.

"Come on. Rest while I get some chores done and dinner together." She led him into the den, helped him onto the couch then switched on the console television in the corner. "Watch some TV."

As the set came on, Gaby retreated to the kitchen, leaving him alone. He wiped his eyes and nose and sunk deeper into the couch, hiding in the shadows.

A news anchor with bad skin and an even worse comb-over sat at a stylish desk, an ACTION NEWS 8 banner on the wall behind him. Decked out in a yellow polyester blazer and ridiculously wide tie, he shuffled a stack of papers and continued relaying a story he'd begun a moment or two earlier. "According to eyewitnesses, the black male exited the bar on Cafferty Boulevard and darted directly into traffic. He was struck by what has been described as a large black sedan, possibly a Ford, which fled the scene. Paramedics are working on the man now and we hope to have a live report from the scene very shortly."

Rooster sat up. The bar he'd met Snow at earlier was on Cafferty Boulevard.

"One eyewitness told Action News 8 the man appeared disoriented and was running as if being chased, though that did not seem to be the case. It's not yet known if the man was intoxicated or under the influence of narcotics, but—one moment…" The anchor put a hand to his ear, listened to the voice in his earpiece then paused for dramatic effect and frowned as if personally devastated. "This just in: the victim, identified as Terrell B. Snow, has been pronounced dead on the scene. As further details become available on this horrific hit-and-run tragedy, we will—"

Rooster turned the television off. The apartment was quiet. He looked to the kitchen. The TV dinners were still on top of the stove but Gaby was nowhere to be found. He hurried through the apartment to the bedroom.

Light filled the room as he flipped the switch. Half-expecting to see the horrible winged and long-tailed creatures in the book flying about, he was relieved to find only shadows, an aged bedroom set and the usual open window. He went directly to the closet and pulled an old shoebox down from the shelf. Inside, a 9mm, a full clip and two boxes of ammunition were wrapped in a cloth. He couldn't remember the last time he'd even touched the gun, much less fired it, but he scooped it up, deftly slapped the clip into place, chambered a round and released the safety. Something about holding the gun steadied his hand.

A cold breeze blew through the room, disturbing the

curtains. He moved to close the window but froze. Beneath a streetlight just beyond the courtyard, a lone man was watching the building.

A priest.

"What's wrong?"

Rooster glanced behind him. Gaby stood in the doorway, a laundry basket of freshly folded clothes in her arms. "How did you know that would be on the news?" he asked.

"How did I know *what* would be on the news?" She noticed his weapon and her face went pale. "Michael, why do you have a gun?"

"Turn off the light," he instructed. "Do it now."

She did. They fell into darkness.

Rooster looked back out the window. The priest was gone.

7

Silence fills the night again.

"Starker's right," Nauls says, "six scarecrows…six of us."

"Not anymore." Landon makes sure he smiles at Snow before he takes the lead, moves by the first scarecrow and heads for the rotting remnants of the old farmhouse. "Scratch one Carbone. Dead guys don't count."

"Before this night's over," Snow mutters, "I'm gonna end that fuck."

The others move on, following Landon now, who has gotten several yards ahead of them and is barely perceptible in the darkness and fog. When they catch up to him, they find themselves standing before a ramshackle two-story structure with a dilapidated porch. To the side of the house and further back on the property is a barn in even worse shape. From the face of the farmhouse, a series of blown-out windows stare down at them, opaque eyes gaping in judgment, perhaps in warning.

A rusted metal sign has been staked a few feet from the front porch steps.

~ KEEP OUT—THIS PROPERTY IS CONDEMNED~

"Yeah," Landon says with a smirk, "didn't see that coming at all."

Rooster immediately feels something so unsettling it leaves him breathless. He squints through the darkness at the looming structure. "I know this place," he hears himself say.

Snow nods, eyes fixed on the house, his mouth hanging open. "So do I."

"Me too," Nauls says, voice shaking.

"Like we've been here before," Starker says.

"Don't worry about it." Landon tests the first step, and once satisfied it will hold his weight, climbs up onto the porch. "These old farmhouses upstate all look alike. You're spooked, that's all. Come on." He ambles across the porch to the front door, which lies on its side next to the doorframe.

"Got to love Landon." Nauls chuckles nervously and climbs the stairs, hoisting the duffel bags of cash along with him. "He ain't afraid of anything."

Snow climbs the steps next. "Too busy being an asshole."

"Let's get this done." Battling uncertainty, confusion and a growing sense of dread, Rooster forces himself up the steps. "I don't want to be here."

Already fearful they will never leave this awful place, Starker, who began in the lead, is the last to enter the house. He joins the others in a large filthy room just inside the entrance. A few broken pieces of what was once furniture are scattered about the otherwise empty area. The floor is rotted in several spots, littered with jagged holes.

Landon sticks the revolver he's been carrying into his belt and pulls free a flashlight. He switches it on, punching a hole in the darkness. Countless dust motes float about in the beam. He sweeps it around. Thick spider webs dangle from the ceiling and fill every corner. A moth flits into the light then spirals off. "Check it out, Nauls. Looks like your apartment, only nicer."

Their movements disturb something in the air, stirring up a pungent odor.

"What the hell is that smell?" Nauls asks, dropping the duffels to the floor and crouching down next to them.

Landon points the flashlight at Snow. "Dude. Seriously. Put your shoes back on."

"You don't get that off me it's going up your ass sideways."

Drifting deeper into the room, Starker watches the ceiling as if expecting something to attack from above. His considerable size causes the floor to creak and shift. He sniffs the air. "It's sulfur."

Nauls opens the first duffel, stares at it dumbly a moment then scrambles to the second one and begins rifling through it. "Landon, put the light here!"

He illuminates the duffels. Both are stuffed with neatly banded pieces of blank paper designed to resemble money.

Snow leans in for a closer look. "Where's the cash?"

"It was here," Nauls says, "I—"

"Unbelievable!" Landon spits. "You assholes stole scrap paper!"

Rooster steps back for a better angle on the others.

Nauls struggles to his feet. "Me and Rooster loaded the cash into the bags. I saw it. It was all there. The bags were full of it."

Landon draws his revolver. "Yeah they're full of it all right." He points it at Rooster. "Where the fuck's my money, crew chief?"

Rooster, Snow and Nauls simultaneously pull their weapons and point them at each other. Preoccupied, and unconcerned with the others, Starker wanders to the back of the room, where a large unusable staircase resides. Littered with broken wood and debris, he gazes up into the shadows of the second-floor. Something dead—probably an animal of some sort, though he cannot be sure—lies in a mangled heap at the very edge of the landing. The walls and upper portion of the banister are streaked with what might be blood.

"Everybody calm down," Rooster says. "We'll figure this out, we—"

"Fuck that," Landon snaps. "Somebody switched out those bags or the money or something and one of you pricks is gonna tell me what's going on or I swear to God I'll shoot every last fucking one of you."

"How could we switch the bags out?" Nauls frantically moves his gun from one person to the next then back again. "They went straight from the armored car to the van, and we were all in the van until we got here. Nobody could switch anything out! We were together the whole time!"

Snow, who has been holding one of his .45s on Landon and the other on Nauls, lowers them both. "He's right."

"I don't give a shit," Landon says. "That money didn't just disappear, so where is it? Rooster, you and Nauls were the ones who loaded it, and since Nauls is a fucking mongoloid, you better start talking."

"Mongoloid?" Nauls cocks an eyebrow. "What the hell is a mongoloid?"

"It's them little elf-looking motherfuckers," Snow explains, "the ones with the pointy heads and shit."

"No, those are cretins," Landon says. "Mongoloids are the redheads."

Nauls tucks his gun into the back of his pants. "I don't have red hair."

Landon sighs but keeps his attention on Rooster, who lowers his weapon as a peace offering. "Get your piece off me," he says, "and we'll figure this shit out."

"Nah, asshole, first you're gonna tell me where the—"

An enormous muscle-bound arm shoots out of the darkness behind him and wraps around Landon's throat, strangling him with such force that his feet leave the ground. He drops his revolver and the flashlight and clutches at the arm with both hands in a futile attempt to dislodge it. The flashlight rolls across the floor, tumbling through the room and painting the farmhouse with sweeping arcs of twisting light that eerily illuminates then plunges each man back into darkness. "Listen to me and listen to me good," Starker says, holding the smaller man effortlessly, his voice just above a whisper in Landon's ear. "We got a lot more to worry about here than that money. Now you cut the shit, keep your mouth shut and do what Rooster tells you to do or I'll snap your neck. You feel me, boy?" Landon manages a gurgling response and Starker releases him. He crashes to the floor with a thud and one of his feet breaks through the boards.

Landon lays there a moment, clutching his throat, then pulls free, retrieves his revolver and slowly returns to his feet without further comment.

Nauls scurries to the corner and retrieves the flashlight. As he brings it round, he stops on something beneath the old staircase. "Hey, there's a—"

"Door under the stairs," Rooster interrupts. He knows he's right but has no idea how he's come to possess such information.

Starker finds Rooster's face in the dark. "It leads to another staircase."

"Then a hallway," Snow says quietly.

"And there's doors on both sides of the hallway," Nauls adds.

Everyone looks to Landon. He rubs at his throat. "Oh I'm allowed to talk now?" He glares at Starker. "Just wanna make sure it's OK with fucking Albert DeSalvo over here before I say anything." Nauls aims the light at him, leaving no doubt that despite his bravado, even Landon is terrified by what's happening. He finally nods reluctantly, fidgeting about tensely. "Yeah, I—I don't know how I know it either, but behind the doors there's a bunch of rooms."

"Even if we're right, end of the day it's just an abandoned old farmhouse with scarecrows out front and some rooms where a cellar ought to be," Snow says. "Why we all so scared?"

"There's only one way to find out for sure."

"Aw, fuck me running." The beam of light begins to tremble as Nauls heads for the porch. "I want out right now, man, this is bullshit."

Starker lifts the AK-47 higher on his hip, and with one short sidestep, blocks the doorway. "We've all been here before. We need to know why."

"But what happened to the money?" Snow asks, his face a mask of barely contained terror.

"Maybe there never was any money," Starker says. "Maybe there wasn't even an armored car."

"Tell that to Carbone," Landon counters. "Fuckhead died robbing it."

"Maybe that's not how he died. Maybe that's just what we remember. Maybe this is all some kind of sick game."

Nauls looks at the floor. "Well I don't wanna play no more."

"Think about what he's saying," Rooster says. "Does anybody really remember anything before the job today?"

"Of course we know what happened today," Landon says.

"Do we?" Rooster watches him, doing his best to keep his face void of emotion. "Do any of you remember anything before the van? Because I'm not sure I do. I mean, I think I do, it feels like I do but…"

"It's in your head," Starker says, "but you don't actually remember *it."*

"Yeah," Snow agrees. "What he said."

Rooster nods.

"So I'm the only one who wants to leave then?" Nauls paces about wildly. "Really? Are you guys fucking high?" The light drifts back and forth across the dark room, cutting shadows and revealing quick glimpses of a long-dead house. In that moment, eyes following the beam, fear wells in Rooster the likes of which he's never known. He's sure he sees something more, something there yet not quite there, waiting in the darkness, slipping from sight like scuttling insects just as the light passes over them. He grips his weapon tighter but it does little to calm his rising terror.

"We need to search this place."

"No we don't." Nauls shakes his head. "We can just leave."

"We need to know what's happening here."

"We can't get upstairs," Starker tells them. "Staircase is blocked with shit and it's all rotted out. But there's something dead up there and whoever killed it did some finger painting with its blood."

"There's something wrong with this place, man, it's—you guys all feel it too, I know you do. Shit Starker you and Rooster felt it outside, and…I don't…" Nauls suddenly becomes strangely calm, his voice quiet and childlike. "I don't want to die out here."

"Easy, Nauls," Landon says. "Don't wanna trip and fall on your vagina."

"Bring the light around to the door under the stairs," Rooster tells him, his gaze moving between the horrified faces before him. "We're going down there."

As daylight splintered night, it brought with it an icy rain that descended upon the city in violent torrents. Shaking off the residue of nightmares, waking and otherwise, Rooster adjusted his position in the chair. He'd placed it in front of the window and watched the street all night. Every muscle in his body hurt, his neck was stiff and sore and his temples pulsed with a dull ache. Ice ticked against the window, mixing with the sluicing rain to blur the glass and world beyond. Numerous lost souls had come and gone throughout the night, hurrying through the darkness, but the priest had not returned. Though he couldn't be certain, Rooster thought he'd briefly nodded off a few times during the night. After asking him countless times to put the gun away and come to bed, Gaby finally gave up a little after midnight and drifted off to sleep. She lay sprawled out across the bed, her breathing slow and deep. He watched her a while. She was the most beautiful woman he'd ever seen. It didn't seem right, Rooster thought, for someone so intelligent, so caring and just, so uncorrupted and faithful to be associated in any way with such madness and horror. Yet somehow it made perfect sense, a pure and tranquil soul like Gaby existing amidst the mayhem, calm beauty at the eye of an otherwise violent storm. His storm.

He sat on the bed next to her and gently caressed her face. She stirred and moaned quietly but remained asleep. *Who are you*? He wondered. *Why are you here with me?*

The pain in his temples drifted behind his eyes, lingering there as he gently kissed Gaby on the cheek. With the 9mm tucked into the back of his pants, he threw on his jacket, swallowed a handful of aspirin and slipped into a cold and unforgiving rain.

8

Rooster found himself standing in the same rain some minutes later, having traced the address on the card to an old restaurant in a long-dead neighborhood. A small dark hole-in-the-wall, it sat alone between a series of boarded-up storefronts and a huge lot of bricks and debris that had once been a building. The street was filthy, cold and lifeless. No cars out in front of the restaurant, but the sign in an otherwise dark window blinked: *Dante's*. There was no one else around, and the second floor above the restaurant appeared deserted, most of the windows blown out or boarded up. Rooster looked to the end of the block, checking the corners in both directions. If he was being watched or tailed, they were the best he'd ever encountered.

He moved through the door, which alerted those inside to his arrival with the jingle of a little bell. His eyes slowly adjusted to the dim lighting as he was met with a blanket of thick, oppressive heat. A series of tables with red-and-white checkered tablecloths and small candles encased in glass orbs at their centers lined the walls to his left and right. The open area between them provided a path through the narrow restaurant to, he assumed, the kitchen in back, but it was so dark he couldn't make out much beyond the first few tables. The smell of burned food hung in the air, and although there was a podium for a maître de the restaurant appeared empty, perhaps closed.

"Here," a voice said from the rear of the room.

Rooster casually slid a hand to the gun in his belt and moved down the center aisle toward the direction of the voice. As the shadows parted, the candlelight danced along the floor and walls, flickering about, alive in the dark. As he cautiously approached the only occupied table in the place, the silhouette of a man's head and shoulders emerged.

"Mr. Cantrell." Not a question. Said with what almost sounded like adoration. "Nasty rain out there this morning."

"Who are you?"

"My name's not important," he said. "Call me whatever you'd like."

Same aged and drained voice as on the phone, Rooster was sure of it.

"Mr. Snow seemed fond of *Poindexter*." The man motioned to the chair across from him with a spindly arm, his hand brushing through the circle of candlelight cast across the table. Skeletal and liver-spotted, his pale flesh was laced with bulbous blue veins, the fingers gnarled with arthritis. "Not terribly original, but we can go with that if you'd like."

"Snow's dead."

"Yes."

Rooster looked behind him. He could see the front door and the light beyond, though it seemed farther away than was possible.

"It's all right, Mr. Cantrell, you're safe here. Please. Sit."

He pulled the chair out, slid it to the side so he could still see the door then took a seat. He'd never cared for sitting with his back to doors. "Who are you?" Rooster pulled his gun and laid it flat on the table, barrel pointed at the man. "I'm not asking again."

Until then the man's face had remained in shadow. He sat forward enough to allow the candlelight to reveal a glimpse of a loose-skinned face ravaged by age, his features sharp and birdlike. A pair of eyeglasses with black frames sat high on his needle nose, the flickering flame from the candle reflected in lenses so thick they might have been comical under different circumstances. "Don't be an ass," he said wearily, "put that away. Our time together is limited."

Rooster reluctantly returned the gun to his lap.

"Are the headaches getting worse?"

He nodded.

"It happens as the mind recovers and remembers more and

more. Truth always comes with some measure of pain." He folded his damaged hands before him on the table and sat back, his face again engulfed in darkness. "Does *The Kingdom Project* mean anything to you?"

Faraway screams tore at him. "No."

"Named for the famous Eliot poem 'The Hollow Men' which speaks of 'death's other kingdom' compiled with numerous books on demonology and the occult that consistently referred to the darkness on the other side as a 'kingdom of shadows,' *The Kingdom Project* was a top secret program begun in the late 1970s and continued until the mid-80s. The occult has always been of interest to the powers that be. Hitler spent a fortune on its study and possibilities. Many of the same scientists that worked for the Third Reich ended up here, in the United States, after World War II. They weren't all rocket scientists, Mr. Cantrell. Many were those who worked on the Reich's most classified occult projects. Their work not only continued here in the states, it expanded and went farther than even Hitler could've imagined."

Outside, the muted sounds of a siren rose then fell away to silence.

"The early programs of the 50s and 60s met with failure," he continued. "For much of the 70s nothing changed, and the majority of programs were scrapped. Many concentrated on psychic phenomenon or the like, but *The Kingdom Project* had different, more sophisticated ideas. Our goal was to discover a connection—a bridge, if you like—between our reality and the underworld. We weren't concerned with an afterlife that could only be entered through death, but rather alternate existences existing simultaneously with ours."

A waiter materialized from the shadows holding a plate of spaghetti and meatballs and a goblet of red wine. He placed them before Poindexter without comment then slipped away.

"I understand you're not a man of science, so I won't bore you with the technical details, but suffice to say it all boils down to physics and mathematics. Our existence, our entire universe, this entire *dimension*, is based upon them. They all are. It's simply a matter of finding the correct equation then executing it via the proper tools. What we as well as the others before us failed to realize was that in a psychological sense, the physical world is essentially an illusion. The path to the other side, to the power we were searching for—the darkness, that place of pure primal terror and evil—isn't something one can find in the depths of the Earth or on a saucer ride through space or any of that nonsense. It exists in the limitless caverns of our minds. Our minds provide the gateway to the other side… the underworld…the darkness. It wasn't Heaven Hitler was searching for, Mr. Cantrell, and neither were we. In the end, these programs all have military—or similar—applications. *The Kingdom Project* was no different. We focused specifically on the dark side of the occult, the concept that things like demons, devils, demonic entities—whatever you'd like to call them—literally existed on some level, if not on a physical plane then perhaps a purely spiritual one. Think about it, beings of pure, unadulterated, unapologetic evil. Beings of pure rage, pure violence, pure hatred. Imagine if that level of evil truly existed in a conscious, intelligent form. Imagine the possibilities of literally summoning such creatures. Imagine harnessing their power, the very essence…of Hell."

"You're out of your fucking mind."

"No, but unfortunately you are. And I'm largely responsible for it." He took up a fork, poked at the food on his plate. "Our push, specifically with *The Kingdom Project,* was largely chemical-based. We believed that once the bridge was found, if it truly existed outside theory and mathematical probability, could only be crossed in a *spiritual* way. In other words, psychologically, as the real-world applications of physics and mathematics had to be merged with spiritual, non-physical, synthetic components."

"Synthetic," Rooster asked, "as in drugs?"

"Yes, and it was only if and when these two areas were in perfect synchronization that our goals could be achieved. The mind itself had to be altered in order to access the other side. There was no question about that. You *could* get there from here, as it were, and the key was right before our eyes. Many ancient cultures, from Native Americans to countless tribes of people worldwide—people we considered largely inferior savages—already possessed the process we'd been searching for. These peoples used it to commune with paradise, to find nirvana, God, peace and transcendence. And they all used mind-altering substances to achieve it—roots, leaves, plants, things of the Earth—ingested before these *journeys* were taken. It's precisely that angle I studied and brought to the project. There were numerous formulas over several years that used pieces of these various concoctions from different cultures. And of course, as a chemist, I implemented my own mixtures, including LSD derivatives and other mind-altering substances. Many did nothing more than standard hits of LSD. The initial versions were far too strong and brought on brain damage, permanent insanity, even death in a few cases. Eventually we were able to isolate the aspects we required and produced what I believed was the perfect elixir for *The Kingdom Project.* Once the right formula was found the challenge became finding proper test subjects. No one sane would knowingly volunteer for such a thing, so we were forced to utilize subjects that hadn't volunteered."

Rooster tightened his grip on the gun but left it in his lap. "You forced people to take a mind-altering drug you cooked up in a test tube?"

"We did. And the results were interesting. Not what we'd hoped for, mind you, but very interesting." He twirled the fork around strands of spaghetti, brought it to his mouth and chewed. "Many subjects experienced something," he said, "but it wasn't the darkness we were searching for. Many believed it was nonsense, false near-death and other psychotic episodes brought on chemically. But I knew this was different. We were so close. The problem, you see, was not with the drug, but the subjects. I began to more closely study the nature of evil, the various interpretations of it in different cultures and varied religions, and though they were often vastly different, I uncovered one consistent thread throughout. According to every doctrine, evil was partly voluntary. One had to embrace it in a sense, allow it. The Devil, if you will, could not simply snatch you up in the dead of night and carry you off to Hell to do with you what he liked. Nor could his minions—demons—attack without provocation, their powers were limited as well. One had to let them 'in' so to speak. Simply put, if the road to Hell truly existed, one could not be dragged there. One had to voluntarily walk that path—through either conscious decision or even outright deception—but one had to allow it. Without that consent, evil could control no man, and no man could find or tap into pure evil. What we needed were not subjects forced into service but rather test subjects that had already embraced the darkness. We tried various subjects that practiced black magic and evil—Satanists and the like—but again met with failure. Evil, it seems, does not want those who so enthusiastically want it. So we began searching prisons. And that is where we found you, Mr. Cantrell. It's where we found all of you. You and your crew were chosen from thousands of potential candidates. You were all condemned, all paying for the horrible crimes you'd committed, all hopeless. If damnation was real, you were all headed straight for it. Murderers, thieves, rapists, terrorists, destroyers of innocents, you were perfect pieces to a larger puzzle of absolute darkness and depravity the likes of which even this hideous world could not begin to comprehend. You were the best of them, granted, the best of the worst, but the best just the same. As it turned out, you were also, however, a rather large fly in the ointment."

Heart smashing his chest, Rooster attempted a deep breath. "You're telling me everything I read in those files is true?"

Poindexter scooped up a forkful of meatball and slid it between his lips. "That is precisely what I'm telling you."

"Why can't I remember?"

"We didn't want you to remember." He wiped a smear of marinara from his chin with a cloth napkin. "So your memories—all your memories—were wiped clean and replaced with memories we wanted you to have."

"Then there was no armored car job?"

"There was not."

"But Carbone, he—he was shot."

"He was killed, yes, but not from a gunshot."

The tremors returned. He struggled to control them. "What then?"

Poindexter rolled more pasta onto his fork, the sauce dripping in thick globs back to his plate. "You remember the farmhouse," he said, the fork shaking in his arthritic hand. "It's coming back to you."

"Yes. Slowly."

"As I mentioned, you were the best of the worst." He stuffed the spaghetti into his mouth. "You tortured and murdered a priest, claiming at your trial that you'd been repeatedly sexually molested by the man when you were a child and that's what had led to your life of crime and eventually his murder. He'd ruined you, and in turn, years later, you had ruined him."

A spike of pain dug deep into his temple and ran down along the right side of his jaw. Rooster fought it back. "I don't…"

"Remember. Yes, I know. For that you should thank me."

"For wiping my memories away and leaving me with lies?"

Ignoring the question, he took up the goblet, sipped some wine. "Of course the pedophilia scandal that shook the Catholic Church had not hit yet."

Rooster had no idea what scandal he was referring to. How much of his mind had these bastards destroyed?

"The idea that a respected, admired and loved parish priest would've ever done such hideous things to a little boy was unthinkable. No one, including us, believed you." Poindexter savored the wine a moment before continuing. "Turns out you were telling the truth, who knew? The fact remained, however, that you tortured and murdered a priest in cold blood. Well done."

"What the hell did you people do to us?"

"We sent you where no human being had ever been before… and returned from." He stabbed another meatball. "You were all given the mixture. It took you to depths none of us could've imagined in our wildest dreams. You went to the core, the heart of evil, to its very soul. I must confess that until that night I hadn't counted on it actually working. But it did. As we'd hoped, you weren't alone in that boundless darkness, there was something else there with you. Something…*alive*."

"Where did we go?"

He grinned like the demons in Rooster's nightmares. "You

touched the face of Lucifer, Mr. Cantrell. And he showed you evil in its purest, most savagely beautiful form, unbridled violence beyond comprehension."

"The farmhouse," Rooster muttered, "the scarecrows, the rooms beneath the house..."

"Props," he said, waving at the air as if to knock the words away. "Familiar images that would elicit fear and discomfort were necessary so the mind would have something to reference. Interesting thing about the human mind, it fills in what is not there, often pulling images from a bank of previous experiences to fill the gaps. We simply helped you all with that, giving you something to experience in a pseudo-physical sense. Something terrifying that you could all relate to and understand."

"This is bullshit." Rooster stood up.

Poindexter continued eating. Candlelight flickered across the plate. The spaghetti was not spaghetti at all, and it was not drenched in tomato sauce. Blood...bile...excrement...worms... human eyeballs cooked to a crisp, burned nearly beyond recognition. "Technically the experiment was a success," he said. "We did achieve what we'd set out to do, at least initially. But then it all went horribly wrong."

"This isn't happening." He pressed his palms to his temples, his head pounding now and his legs weak. "This isn't...this isn't..."

"Once we realized what we'd truly tapped into, that it was the equivalent of accessing the literal power of existence, and the dark side of existence at that, we knew we'd overestimated our abilities. It was actually quite beautiful in its purity, but you were all torn to shreds by its profane glory. It became an orgy of violence and blood, an orgy of death."

"You're lying, you sonofabitch." Rooster pointed the 9mm at him.

"Do you really think we could let any of you come back at that point? Or that there'd be anything left to bring back?"

"Then where am I? I'm standing right here!"

"The longer you struggle against truth, the longer the forces of darkness will bind you, Mr. Cantrell. There are some things human beings can never control. We're not meant to, regardless of how badly we may desire it. Evil—true evil—is one of those things. I understand it's hard for you to accept, but you were all thoroughly expendable, Mr. Cantrell, a bunch of hooligans and lowlifes, losers and drains on society no one cared about then or now."

"It wasn't enough that you used us as guinea pigs for your demented projects, crippled our minds and broke us to pieces. You had to wipe out our memories and send us back into the world haunted by nightmares you put there and with no knowledge of who we are or how we got here? You destroyed us—you admit it—and yet you still try to cover it up with bullshit stories about demons and Hell and—"

"Do you really believe telling yourself that long and hard enough will keep the terror at bay?" Poindexter placed the fork next to the plate and wiped the blood from his mouth with the napkin. "You all disappeared from the face of the Earth and not a single person noticed, much less cared."

"Then why come to us after all this time?"

"Penance," he said softly, the air of arrogance fading. "It's what's required of me now. Eventually, we all serve one master or another, Mr. Cantrell, whether we like it or believe in it or not. And I've come to learn that it rarely turns out to be the one we were counting on."

"Who are the men that killed Snow, the men in the Crown Vic?"

He smiled blandly. "They're not men."

"What do I do?" Rooster leaned across the table so that the gun was only a few inches from the man's face. "How do I kill these things in my head?"

He leaned further into the light, pulled his glasses from his pale and sickly face and pushed forward until his forehead met the barrel of the gun. "Deliver me from my sins," he whispered. "Deliver *us* from evil."

Rooster's finger remained remarkably steady as it curled to the trigger.

The old man's eyes rolled to white. Everything else turned crimson.

9

The flashlight beam slides along the dirty floor to the door under the stairs. An inverted pentagram has been painted across it in blood. Above it and to the left, also in blood, are the numbers 666 and a series of words Rooster cannot decipher.

"Oh hell *no, that's Devil shit right there." Snow backs away.*

Rooster studies the words scrawled on the door. "What language is that?"

"Latin."

They all look to Starker. The giant shrugs. "I took it in high school you ignorant motherfuckers."

"What's it mean?"

"Abandon Hope All Ye Who Enter Here." Starker finds Rooster in the darkness behind him. "Supposedly that's what it says at the gates of Hell."

"Why would somebody put that there?" Nauls asks in a panic.

"Probably a bunch of drugged-out, loser, never been laid, douche bag, Devil-worshipping-wannabes." Landon pushes past the others. "Who gives a shit? If we're doing this let's get it over with."

With that, Starker steadies his stance then kicks in the door. It implodes and tears from its hinges with a loud cracking, splintering sound, tumbling away into darkness down another set of stairs. They hear it land seconds later as an enormous cloud of dust and dirt kicks up in response, wafting out the open doorway and bursting into the room. A stale mildew odor is followed by a pungent smell similar to rotting garbage and raw sewage. They cough, block their nostrils then huddle together in the limited light until the stench weakens and the farmhouse is returned to eerie silence.

No one speaks, but before anyone can motion Nauls to lead the way with the flashlight, he hands it to Rooster. With a sigh, Rooster takes the lead, the light in one hand and his 9mm in the other. He steps through, aims the light and sees a small set of wooden stairs. Beyond them is a cement landing and what appears to be a corridor he and the others were somehow already aware of.

He begins his descent. Starker is behind him, his weight shaking the staircase with each step. Next is Landon. Snow and Nauls pull up the rear.

They reach the corridor without incident. Rooster pans the light along the walls. Several doors line either side. The far end of the hallway is draped in a darkness that the flashlight is unable to penetrate from this distance. The fear and danger is palpable now, a spiritual entity unmistakably alive and horrific, real, it drifts and moves around them like liquid, invisible to the naked eye but without question, present. Rooster sweeps the light along one wall and then the next, as together, the crew slowly moves deeper into the corridor. All the doors are closed.

Except one. He places the light on it. This door is ajar. Rooster uses hand motions to let the others know what needs to be done. He sends Starker to the left side of the doorway, Snow to the right. Rooster then crouches, facing the door head-on while Landon covers his back and Nauls watches the section of hallway and stairs behind them.

Starker holds the AK-47 in one hand and raises the other into the light so everyone can see. Slowly, he counts off, raising one finger, then another and finally a third. A quick nod, and the crew springs into action, rushing into the room with weapons at the ready and the flashlight leading the way.

Silence returns. A mocking silence…

The light trembles in Rooster's hand. But they see.

They all see.

A series of metal slabs like something out of a coroner's workshop, bodies atop them in hospital johnnies, IVs attached to their arms pumping some clear fluid into their veins, oxygen tubes implanted in their nostrils, wires running from their heads and chests and limbs to machines and computers along the far wall, all of it organized and functioning in the dark bowels of an abandoned farmhouse in the middle of nowhere. Six metal tables. Six men.

"God in Heaven," someone says in a desperate whisper. "It's us."

It might've been hours, might've been days. He could no longer tell the difference.

The rain had stopped and the air was still, but it had gotten much colder. Bundled in a heavy coat and knit hat, the briefcase in his free hand, Rooster stood arm-in-arm with Gaby before a fresh grave. Dressed in a black dress and heels, her face partially covered with a lace veil, moments before she had placed flowers where a headstone should've been. Her lips moved in silent prayer behind the veil, dark eyes lowered. No one else was there. A life, Snow's life, had ended. Here, at this unmarked grave. And no one cared. It was like he'd never really been there at all.

Gaby finished her prayers, and together, they turned to leave.

It was then that Rooster saw them. Across the sea of headstones, crypts and monuments to the dead, two men watched them, their breath converted to spiraling clouds rising from their bodies like fleeing souls.

Gaby saw them, too. "Do what you have to do." She lifted the veil, rose up on her toes so she could reach, and kissed his cheek. "I love you."

As she moved away toward the gates of the cemetery, the men started toward him. Rooster lit a cigarette and smoked it until they reached him.

They looked the same.

Landon stared at him, said nothing.

"Hey, Rooster," Nauls offered, scratching at his beard and smiling nervously, eyes concealed behind the usual sunglasses. "Good to see you, bro."

"Good to see you too, Nauls."

"That is *so* precious—seriously—I think I just tinkled a little. How about we save the group hug for later and you two can finish jerking each other's gherkins then, OK?" Landon stepped closer. "Paper said the hit-and-run was probably an accident, driver just panicked. I say kiss my celluloid-dimpled ass, whoever hit Snow did it on purpose. Can't blame them—I would've run the prick over if he stepped in front of my car too—but sounds like somebody took him out to me."

Rooster took a final drag on his cigarette then dropped it and crushed it out with his boot. "They did."

"Do you know who *they* are?"

"I'm not sure yet, but—"

"You heard about Starker?"

"Snow said he killed his old lady and ran to Mexico."

"He never got that far. Big bastard was hiding out in a fleabag motel right here in the city. They found him a few weeks back, in the bathtub, wrists slashed clear to the bone. Sorry, I'm not buying that one either. Same fuckers probably did him too."

"I keep having these dreams," Nauls blurted out. "Nightmares, I—"

Landon held a hand up like a crossing guard. "Let the grownups talk."

"Fuck you, man! You're having them too. Tell him. *Tell him.*"

Landon defiantly bit his lip and looked away.

"Rooster," Nauls said, barely able to contain his tears, "I've been having these dreams. There's all this screaming and yelling and blood and horrible shit. Then it gets dark and I can't see. I can't move, I can't even breathe and it feels like I'm being smothered. I try to open my mouth to scream only I can't. My mouth, it's—somebody's *sewn* it shut. Who would—the bad dreams won't stop, they—I'm even starting to have them when I'm awake, I—"

"We all are," Rooster said evenly.

Nauls ran a hand through his tangle of hair. "Every time I leave the house I see this chick and this older dude, they're dressed like they work in an office or a bank or something and they follow me and want to talk to me, but there's something not right about them. They look so familiar only I don't know who they are. And Landon, he—he don't drive no more. *Landon* don't drive. He can't. Every time he gets behind the wheel of a car he sees this lady holding a baby."

"She's on every fucking corner just staring at me." Landon became visibly shaken as his resistance fell away. "I know her from somewhere but…I'm pretty sure the baby's dead."

"What's happening?" Nauls asked. "What happened to us that night at the farmhouse? We can't remember nothing but bits and pieces."

"I've got something to show you," Rooster said softly, as if the dead might otherwise hear. He held up the briefcase.

"What's that?"

"The truth."

"This isn't possible," Landon mumbles.

As if in a trance, Snow approaches the last table, the only one covered with a white sheet which has apparently been thrown there to conceal Carbone's body. "Carbone's dead," he says. "He's dead, and he's back in that van."

Mesmerized, the others gawk at their likenesses on the tables before them, confusion and fear igniting as one and slashing at them like razorblades. Rooster cocks his head, studying his own face just feet away, eyes closed and face void of expression as if in the throes of a deep, drug-induced sleep.

Inches from the covered metal table, Snow pokes at the sheet with one of his .45s. The sheet begins to shake in response, as whatever lies beneath convulses. Horrified, Snow yanks back the sheet.

Sans Johnny, wires and tubes, Carbone's nude body lies quivering violently on the table. His lower abdomen and sexual organs are ripped to shreds, and the remainder of his body has sustained thousands of small but horribly deep serrated cuts, as if it's been wrapped in barbed wire then torn free. The lacerations, many blackened and scabbed over, others fresh and still bleeding, form a crisscross pattern on his savaged skin that is as strangely alluring in its symmetry as it is appalling in its brutality.

As Snow backs away, both .45s locked on the body, Carbone suddenly sits up, vaulting forward. His eyes open but they are empty raw sockets. He continues to spasm uncontrollably in seizure. "He's coming." His voice is no longer exclusively his own, but many, and sounds as if it is stacked atop countless others, giving it an unsettling echolike, inhuman tone. "He's coming..."

Hands to his ears, Nauls stumbles back into the hallway like a terrified child.

"Shoot it!" Landon screams. Snow is frozen in place.

"He knows who we really are," it says. "He knows the things we've done. Our secrets, he knows them all. He's coming..."

"God help us," Rooster mutters.

"God?" Carbone turns what remains of his butchered face in the direction of Rooster's voice. His split lips curl into a hideous, bloody-toothed grin.

Starker levels the AK-47 and unloads.

The discharge is deafening in such an enclosed space, and sends the body tumbling from the metal slab. It crashes to the floor as if boneless, flesh slapping cement floor as the impact empties the remains of its internal organs from the body cavity.

From the corridor behind them, Nauls begins to scream.

At the outskirts of the city, on a lonely dirt road, Rooster leaned against Nauls' car and smoked a cigarette. He'd waited as Nauls and Landon poured over the material in the briefcase, then he answered their questions as best he could. Both men exchanged uncertain glances throughout, and now stood watching Rooster as if expecting him to tell them what to do next.

"They used us like lab animals," Rooster finally said. "They wiped our minds clean, and now that we're starting to remember they're taking us out one by one. They figure they can toss us aside like garbage."

"We are garbage," Nauls replied quietly.

"Maybe so, but we never even got the chance to make things right, to—"

"What?" Landon interjected. "*Repent*? Save our souls? Deliver ourselves from evil like this Poindexter dude told you?"

Rooster stared at him.

"Maybe that's exactly what we're doing right now," Landon said.

A breeze blew past, causing nearby trees to whisper and sway.

"We have to go back," Rooster said.

"To the farmhouse, are you serious?" Landon gave a wry smile. "You want to go *back* there?"

Rooster nodded, smoke curling around his head like creeping vines. "You think you could find it again after all this time?"

"Yeah." Landon looked to Nauls but he had his back to him. "I can find it."

He hadn't expected Landon to be so adamant. But then he hadn't expected his and Nauls' nearly blasé reaction to the things he'd told them either. Something had changed since they'd driven out here. The moment he'd agreed to go with them they no longer seemed quite as upset as they'd been initially. He dropped his cigarette and pushed away from the car. "You're sure?"

"Rooster, I…*we've*…been there since."

"You've been back there since that night?"

"You don't understand," Landon said. "We never left."

Running…screams…confusion…Panic explodes through the darkness…

The flashlight bounces, throwing strobe-like splashes of light along the corridor, floors, walls and ceiling before finally settling on Nauls. His face protrudes from the darkness, eyes closed but with a look of horrific pain. Blood slowly trickles from his nostrils into his beard.

The others scramble about trying to cover the corridor. Landon frantically knocks Snow out of the way and climbs the stairs back to the house.

Nauls opens his eyes. "He's here," he says in a loud whisper.

His body begins to shake. Slowly at first but gradually building in intensity, he begins to buck, wracked with increasingly violent spasms. His thin frame twists as he flails about, and his weapon falls to the floor. He brings his shaking hands to his face, screams and stabs his fingers directly into his eyes.

Rooster reaches out in an effort to stop him, but it's too late.

Nauls tears his eyes from their sockets with a spray of blood and fluid, his screams replaced with laughter as his spasms grow worse and he begins to spin like a top.

"Jesus God!" Snow shrieks, falling away in horror.

"Go!" Starker grabs Snow and throws him toward the stairs. "Go!"

Rooster stands paralyzed, holding the flashlight on Nauls, who comes to rest, laughing through the blood and pain, holding an eyeball in each hand as if in offering, hideous moist strings dangling from them and dripping blood. "We're going where there are no eyes," he says, his voice little more than a garbled growl now. "Where everyone is blind… yet everyone sees."

Blood suddenly spews from his mouth, eye sockets, nose and ears. Like something has exploded deep inside him, the blood sprays free as his screams return, this time as raspy, animal-like squeals. "He's here," he gurgles, choking on the blood as it pours out over his bottom lip. "He's—"

Nauls flies backwards, crashes into the far wall like he's been thrown by something savage and powerful. His body slides to the floor, swallowed by the shadows there.

Rooster feels Starker's enormous hand clamp onto his arm and yank him back just before he fires a burst from the AK-47 into the darkness. Together, they run for the stairs. "Don't look back!" Starker yells out.

But it no longer matters.

The darkness, and all that dwells within it, follows.

In the room upstairs, Snow lurches about, lost in the dark, his guns at his side and his mouth open, soundlessly forming words—perhaps prayers—while something speaks to him from the surrounding shadows only he can hear. The voice of a woman, a young woman asking him why, her voice oddly hollow as she shuffles about nearby, hidden in darkness, her breath cold and rapid on the back of his neck. But when Snow turns there is only night, moonlight and fog beyond the blown-out windows. The scarecrows watch a field of weeds, a dead forest and a path to nowhere, an empty road no one will ever cross again.

The voice, different now—neither male nor female and no longer entirely human—whispers his name.

Snow wants to run for the door but can't move. He knows, understands for the first time, what is coming, and still cannot move. He trembles and begins to urinate. As the .45s drop from his hands the fire appears from nowhere, sweeping over the ceiling then down the wall and across him, engulfing his body in seconds. Oddly, Snow feels no burning sensation, no pain, only sorrow and hopelessness the depths of which he never believed possible. He stumbles, flaming arms and hands held out in front of him as if to embrace some invisible presence. He sinks to his knees. Eyes wide, he stares at something through the growing inferno and laughs maniacally.

The last thing Snow sees is Starker and Rooster rushing up the stairs.

Outside, Landon runs with all his might, the tall grass and overgrown weeds slowing him as he wades toward the road. The van, *he thinks,* just have to make it to the van and I'm free. *He ignores the scarecrows' dead stares and does not look back, even when he's certain there is something right behind him, closing in with impossible speed and ready to swoop down and pluck him from the field like a hawk closing in on a mouse. He bolts through the last bit of field and jumps the final embankment down to the road. Pitching forward on landing, he catches himself, and now on pavement, takes a quick look back. No one coming, nothing behind him. He pulls the revolver from his belt just in case, sees the farmhouse in the distance. It's on fire, the flames creeping up through the roof, lapping night. He turns and runs for the van but pulls up short after only a few strides. It's gone. He looks around frantically. This isn't possible. He parked it there himself, out of the way, just as Rooster instructed.*

"Yeah, I need this shit." He heads off down the road, running right down the center lane through the darkness; the fog-shrouded moon his only guide. Every now and then he looks back. The farmhouse, the scarecrows and the fire grow fainter and fainter until the night swallows them whole and he is alone in the darkness.

He slows his pace a few minutes later, finally opting for a fast walk. His chest heaves as he tries to catch his breath and a sharp pain digs at his side. Landon keeps moving, knowing eventually he's bound to run into something—a car, a house—anything. He notices a slight incline to the road. He pushes on, trying to forget the things he saw back there. All he needs is a car. He can hotwire anything and be long gone from this place for good. He kicks it back up a notch, jogging up and over the sloped portion of road. In the distance, he sees an outline of a building. Set back quite a distance from the road, it is merely a silhouette, but a hulking one. Must be a house, *he reasons, then increases speed and veers off pavement onto grass.*

Running across the field, he watches it become more and more defined the closer he gets. Within minutes Landon realizes it's a barn.

Beyond it is a farmhouse.

A farmhouse guarded by scarecrows…a farmhouse in flames.

"No fucking way." He comes to a stop between the barn and the house. He's gone in a circle, but how is that possible? He ran straight and in the opposite direction the entire time.

Shadows drift through the weeds before him. Landon steps back and raises the revolver. He can hear screams and smells a suspicious burning odor. Beyond that of burned wood, it is sickeningly sweet and similar to the stench of charred meat.

A baby cries somewhere nearby. Landon whirls in the direction to find only darkness. Blind with terror, he runs but trips over something and pitches forward into the grass and dirt. He scrambles to his feet, sees what he fell over. A wooden stake…a cross of wood…

The scarecrow, *he thinks, his mind shattering.* It's gone.

From behind him, shuffling movement.

A strange shape comes toward him through the tall grass, hobbling like a crippled man.

Only this is not a man.

Landon fires the revolver. Keeps firing even when the revolver is empty and makes only clicking sounds.

And then something coarse covers his head, cold dead hands wrap around his throat and he hears another scream shred the night, unaware that this one is his own.

In the farmhouse, Starker and Rooster run through the burning front room, trying to find a way out in all the madness and confusion.

The darkness is alive, shifting and thick with the shrieking cries of countless dead, nameless lost souls all wailing in the night with violent fury. Rooster sees a pillar of fire and realizes it is Snow kneeling before them, his body wrapped in blankets of flame.

Like a cold winter wind, something follows them up the stairs, gusts into the room and cuts through them. It feeds the flames and Snow's body becomes a firestorm. Yet he doesn't topple. Instead he struggles slowly to his feet.

Rooster shoots him, emptying his gun.

Snow finally topples over and the fire spreads, racing up the walls and along the floor in search of more victims.

The strange wind passes, surging out to the field beyond the doorway, and Rooster feels some part of himself go with it. He stumbles after it, dazed and fighting the gripping cold suddenly rising from the depths of his body. He finds Starker standing next to Snow's body, staring at it with a strange look of…satisfaction? He throws the AK-47 aside, drops down, and eyes ablaze with passion claws at the burned heap that had once been Snow, ripping charred meat in stringy handfuls he hungrily devours.

And as the fire spreads, Rooster understands. He feels it too. Lust not for sex but violence, death, mayhem, destruction and pain…as if these things have been his destiny all along. Rather than reload the 9mm, he drops it and reaches for a combat knife tucked in his boot. He slides it free, already salivating as he closes on Starker.

Behind him, Nauls slowly ascends the stairs, his hollow eyes piercing the smoke and darkness, his mouth twisted into a hideous demonic smile.

Rooster slams the blade deep into Starker's lower back, pulls it free and stabs him again. He seems not to notice at first, but then collapses from his knees to his side and lies there laughing, his large teeth bright in the darkness and caked with blood and human flesh.

As Rooster sets to work on him, gutting Starker from throat to pelvis, Nauls moves past, through the fire and out the doorway to the field.

His feet do not touch the floor.

Rooster focuses on Starker's laughter. No—not laughter—not anymore, cries now, screams. Beautiful screams…his face and bald head covered in blood as he spits and slobbers, each scream more horrific than the last. As Rooster tears at the enormous incision then plunges his hands inside the body, Starker chokes on the bodily fluids bubbling up into his throat and begs for mercy.

But all Rooster hears are the shrieks of souls trapped in the darkness and flames surrounding him.

Cords of intestines clutched in one hand and the knife in the other, he leaves Starker's now silent but convulsing body and slowly approaches the doorway. Darkness waits…a field of tall grass and weeds…six wooden crosses…three with fresh scarecrows nailed to them…three still waiting…

Rooster begins to laugh, bringing the intestines to his lips and eating as he steps out of the flames and into the night.

Somewhere within the hurricane of violence and howling souls, a frantic, familiar and decidedly human voice screams for salvation.

Visions of demonic creatures—some human, some not, and others still stranded at various horrific points between the two—flashed through his mind. Held in rusty metal cages, pinned, strapped or chained to medieval devices of torture and imprisonment, the creatures gawked at him in horror, several deathly still, others violently struggling to free themselves, all of them moist with blood, urine and excrement, their bodies grotesquely deformed and savaged.

The terrifying chambers of blood and death dissolved; became a roadside.

Landon had already gone quite a ways up the incline on the side of the road and looked back as if he expected Rooster to follow. But Rooster knew now what lay on the other side of the tall grass blowing in the wind behind him.

With a shrug, Landon held his arms out like the victim of crucifixion and backed away over the ridge, vanishing from sight.

Nauls turned to him, removed his sunglasses.

We're going where there are no eyes…

His eyes were gone, just empty sockets.

Where everyone is blind…yet everyone sees.

Without warning his body shook with impossible velocity, transforming him into little more than a blur before he again fell still. "Come with us," Nauls said.

"We'll all figure this out together."

Rooster shook his head no.

Nauls slid his sunglasses back on, slowly walked up the embankment after Landon then hesitated and looked back. "You really think you have a choice?"

"That's all any of us have."

Nauls reached into his jacket pocket, pulled free the car keys and tossed them to Rooster. "We'll be waiting," he said sadly. "Forever."

10

He made the car tailing him even before he'd reached his apartment. Rooster pulled over a block from the housing projects and continued on foot. As he crossed the courtyard, hurrying through the cold, the black Crown Vic crept slowly past, the windows and windshield impenetrably tinted. It continued a bit further down the street then pulled over and parked. Rooster kept checking back over his shoulder, but no one emerged from the vehicle.

When he'd reached his floor, Rooster stopped at the incinerator shoot and dropped the briefcase in, listening to it slide away down the shaft to the fires below.

Burn, he thought. *Burn in Hell.*

He slipped into the apartment and was met by a welcome burst of heat. Moving silently, he went to the bedroom and stopped just inside the doorway. Gaby was standing next to the bed, a blanket in her arms and a laundry basket at her feet. She'd already stripped the comforter, blanket and top-sheet from the bed but the bottom sheet remained. She seemed surprised to find him there, but smiled anyway. It was perhaps the most reassuring and comforting thing he'd ever seen.

Until he took a closer look at the bed. Rich dark soil was scattered across the sheet, blood and straw along the pillows. He narrowed his eyes and grimaced as fear clawed at what few defenses he had left.

"It's all right," Gaby said, quickly tossing the blanket over the bed. "Don't look. It doesn't mean anything. They're just trying to frighten you."

The night sky rolled above, moving, the fog turning and twisting as the rough ground tore at his back and shoulders.

"Gaby," he said softly, voice breaking. "Gabrielle…help me."

They were dragging him by his legs…pulling him across the field, the grass and weeds tangling and scratching him as he went, the night sky overhead, vast and ominous, the smell of death and burning flesh filling the air.

"Hell does more than burn the wicked," she said. "It cleanses the lost clawing for the light. Remember what I told you. Let me help you tear them apart like they've torn at you."

Hideous hands of straw, of charred flesh and exposed bone held him down against the fallen cross of wood while shadows moved about, laughing horribly even as they drove nails through his palms, destroying flesh and shattering bone, even as they hoisted the cross up and into position, even as Rooster screamed and begged for God to save him, even as unseen filthy hands held his mouth closed while others pierced his lips with an old rusted needle, running the leather string through the holes and pulling it taut until his screams were muffled groans and his mouth could no longer open.

"Remember what I told you," she said again.

Those in the shadows pulled the burlap sack over his head, two holes cut out in the fabric to accommodate his eyes. Eyes that could still see…inhuman eyes now, the eyes of a soulless scarecrow… impossible eyes opening, seeing, watching, frozen in time, crucified to damnation and endless suffering.

"Rooster," Gaby said forcefully, "remember what I told you about my name and what it means. Do you remember?"

"God is my might."

And his eyes see the Hell he is trapped in…a Hell not of demons with pitchforks and cloven-hooves or boundless oceans of fire…but one in a small bedroom not so different than the one Rooster stood in now. A quiet and dark room where a little boy sat on a bed with crisp white sheets, crucifixes on the walls and a devil he'd believed a god sitting next to him whispering assurances that the things happening were just and right and moral and clean. Father McKay staring down at him with those striking blue eyes and telling him everything would be all right if he simply obeyed God's will.

Tears stain Rooster's cheeks. Rage, sorrow, fear—he cannot decide. All of them, goddamn you, all of them in a tempest of blood and tears and evil.

"They're dying. You're killing them one by one." Gaby motioned to him with a slight turn of her head, her beauty shifting to something decidedly more sinister. "Burn them. Burn the *fuckers* away like the leeches they are."

He smelled death...dirt...an open grave and its rotting remains...

Terror strangled him, its grip desperate.

The priest stood behind him, filthy and discarded now, like the souls he'd torn from countless children years before. "I know you," he said.

"I watched you die." Visions of Starker came to him. No. Not Starker. Father McKay, his head drenched in blood, choking on his own body fluids and gasping for forgiveness. "I killed you. Slowly."

Blood so dark it was nearly black trickled from the corners of his eyes. "Did you think that would save your soul?" the priest asked.

"I only knew it would end you."

The priest moved deeper into the room, stepping between him and Gaby, smiling wide like a demonic Cheshire Cat. "But that's what you hoped for, wasn't it. Just like now, you hope it will save you from me, from this place, from those waiting for you outside, from yourself. It won't. Do you know why?" A fat brown spider scurried across his bald head, disappeared into his ear. He didn't seem to notice. "Because the illusion of hope is Hell's greatest joy."

"And Heaven's greatest weapon," Gaby said from behind him, her eyes rolling to black as she grabbed hold of him, sunk her teeth into his neck and pulled him to the floor with shocking strength and violence, straddling him and tearing at his throat the way a wild dog might.

Light and dark merged as blood sprayed the walls. Rooster backed away until he'd vanished into the safety of nearby shadows, the meager scraps of sanity he still possessed fracturing as night fell over the city of the damned.

Lost in time, through bloodshot eyes Rooster watched the sun rise on a new day, broken dreams collected at his feet, tarnished trophies stolen rather than won. The beautiful innocence of a little boy nailed to a cross of wood in burning fields called to him across the years, tears from a forgotten and wasted life and the sins of ghosts from a past he couldn't quite remember and perhaps never would. Perhaps he wasn't meant to.

Repent? Save our souls? Deliver ourselves from evil? But rather than destroy, the flames in those burning fields were what would eventually free him.

Maybe that's what we're doing right now.

Rooster rubbed his hands together, they'd gone so cold. He lit a Marlboro and checked the corner. The Crown Vic was gone. From behind him, he heard heels clacking pavement. Bundled in a winter coat and hat, Gaby walked across the courtyard with her typical brisk stride.

Across the street, Nauls' car waited. Gaby smiled, no longer wolf, but lamb. "Where are we going?" Rooster asked.

"Away from here," she said, offering him her hand.

"Home?" he asked.

"Home," she said. "But get rid of the cigarette. Those things'll kill ya."

He slipped his hand into hers, and for the first time in a long while, felt himself smile.

Fires burned. They always would. But Rooster's flames no longer trapped him in a Hell of his or anyone else's creation. Instead, they destroyed those things shackling him to the Devil's playground, and all the nightmares and lies that had tried so desperately to keep him there.

The longer you struggle against truth…

In a dark and distant field, a hideous scarecrow closed its sightless eyes.

The longer the forces of darkness will bind you…

Rooster's soul quieted as the demons fell back into the lightless abyss from which they'd come.

Hand-in-hand with Gaby, Rooster walked to the car.

Somewhere beyond the horizon, death's other kingdom waited.

A kingdom not of shadows and darkness, but of peace.

SORCERER

"Evil is obvious only in retrospect."

—Gloria Steinem
Outrageous Acts and Everyday Rebellions

1

"He's still out there."

As he sat up, Jeff's perspiration-soaked back peeled away from the bed sheet. He squinted drowsily at the clock on the nightstand. The numbers were a jumbled blur. "What are you doing up?"

"I couldn't sleep." Perhaps carelessly, Eden stood nude at the apartment window. "I needed something cold to drink." She held up a bottle of water in evidence. "It's after midnight and he's still out there."

"Of course he is." Jeff swung his feet to the floor.

"That's where he lives."

"It's ridiculous. No one should be living on the streets in this day and age."

"I'd call the cops," he said through a yawn, "but they won't do anything."

"Why would calling the police be your first reaction? He's not doing anything wrong. He's not a criminal, Jeff, he's homeless."

"Let him be homeless someplace else."

"Don't be so cruel." Eden ran the cool plastic bottle across her brow and down along her flushed cheek. "He's harmless."

"How would you know?"

"He *seems* harmless, OK?"

"The guy's probably a drunk or a drug addict—maybe both—and there's a good chance he's mentally ill. Most of them are, you know."

"Well I feel sorry for him," she muttered.

"Bums are bums for a reason. They're usually bad news,

these guys. For all we know he could have a criminal record a mile long."

"And he could just as easily be someone who caught a couple bad breaks and found himself out on the street."

Jeff searched the nightstand, located his eyeglasses and slipped them on. "Jesus, get out of the window."

"It's dark, he can't see in."

"No wonder he's been trying to talk to you lately."

Eden pushed a wisp of short brown hair from her eyes. "If you don't get a job soon we'll be out there with him. And then people like you can say horrible things about us too."

"People like me?"

"You used to be a lot more compassionate."

"That's when I could afford to be. I don't see anybody helping us, do you? We're all on our own in this life."

"And here I thought we had each other."

"You know what I mean."

"Not sure I do, actually."

"Don't turn this into an argument, OK?"

Eden delicately placed her free hand flat against the screen, as if to touch the night itself, or perhaps escape into it. "The bills are piling up."

"I'll take care of it."

She faced him, pale breasts cutting the darkness. "If something doesn't break soon—"

"I said I'd take care of it." Jeff stood, peeled his boxers from his thighs and headed out of the room. "I need some aspirin."

Eden looked back at the street two stories below. The man huddled at the base of their steps was watching her. He *could* see her, and they both knew it. For reasons unknown even to her, Eden felt inexplicably drawn to him ever since he'd first appeared on their street a few days before. Ignoring the rapid beat of her heart and the tingling in her nipples as they slowly stiffened, she wiped a trickle of sweat from between her breasts but made no move to cover them. The man gazed up at her, a crippling sorrow filling his eyes as he slid one hand down the front of his soiled pants.

She held his stare with an impassive version of her own.

The man's hand moved slowly at first and then more quickly. He nodded at her, encouraging her to take it farther, his hand jerking furiously now. She could see his lips moving but couldn't hear what he was saying, just vague whispers in the night.

The man took a quick look up then down the avenue. No traffic, no one else on the street. As his stare returned to her, he unzipped his pants and pulled his erection free, stroking himself in plain view.

She stared at what he'd exposed, knowing it turned him on.

A throaty moan escaped him, echoed along the otherwise empty street.

Eden closed her eyes. A shiver breached the stifling heat and coursed through her. Absently, she dropped a hand to her upper thigh, fingertips just inches from the soft mound of pubic hair and the beginnings of wetness between her legs.

"I've got a splitting headache." Jeff's voice snapped her back as he returned to the bedroom. "Not sure if it's allergies or what."

She casually slid her hand up onto her waist. "It's probably stress," she managed, clearing her throat.

Jeff sat on the edge of the bed and watched shadows slink along the smooth contours of his wife's bare back. Glistening with perspiration, her flesh looked like it had been sprayed down with a fine mist. "I was having a dream," he told her. "Just now, before I woke up."

"What was it about?"

"I was here, in the city, but I was lost and I couldn't find you. It was like I had no memory of the city at all. I just kept aimlessly wandering the streets looking for you. I looked everywhere, but I couldn't find you."

"It's OK," she said softly. "I'm right here."

Eden opened her eyes. The homeless man was gone.

2

Jeff left the apartment earlier than usual. As he exited through the main doors at the end of a small lobby, he saw the man sitting on the front steps. His clothes were filthy and ragged, his thinning dark hair snarled and matted, and the scraps of material covering his feet just barely qualified as shoes.

"Excuse me," Jeff said firmly, "but I've asked you not to hang around here. If you keep it up I'll have to call the police, understand?"

The man looked at him through bloodshot eyes and scratched at the heavy growth of stubble along his chin. "Why do you hate me?" he asked in a raspy voice.

Eden's face came to him just then, her words from the night before ringing in his ears. *You used to be a lot more compassionate.* Jeff continued to the bottom step. "Look," he said, attempting a considerate tone, "I don't hate you, all right? But you make a lot of people in the building uncomfortable."

"Then how come you're the only one who gives me a hard time? I've never done anything to you."

"Don't you have anywhere else to go?"

"If I had anywhere but the street, don't you think I'd be there?"

Jeff found himself studying the man closely for the first time. They were roughly the same age, middle thirties, and he couldn't help but wonder how things might've been different had their lives taken even slightly altered courses. Maybe they'd have been friends or colleagues, or maybe their roles would've been reversed. "Isn't there anyone who can help you get on your feet?"

"I wasn't born like this you know." The man did his best to smooth his hair into place with his grimy hands. "I used to have everything you've got, things just went bad. It happens."

Jeff reached for his wallet. "Listen, I just lost my job recently so I'm not in a position to do much, but let me give you a few bucks. Go get a bite to eat and clean up a little."

The man stared at the twenty in Jeff's hand. "I don't want your money."

"Just take it and go, all right?" Jeff thrust it at him a second time.

The man struggled to his feet and slowly walked away.

Whatever, Jeff thought. *I tried.* He returned the money to his wallet and started off in the opposite direction along Massachusetts Avenue. Their apartment, located in Boston's Back Bay, was only a few blocks from the Boston Commons public park. Their neighborhood consisted largely of residential three-story walkups sandwiched one against the next that catered mostly to long-term tenants or college kids renting apartments from local college-owned buildings. But for the nearly constant traffic along the avenue, it was a nice area, though one Jeff couldn't be sure how much longer they'd be able to afford.

He turned at the corner and continued on until he'd reached Boylston Street. There he stopped at a newsstand, bought a *Boston Globe* then crossed the busy intersection leading to Copley Square, a large cement park between the Hancock Tower, a shopping complex and several enormous old churches. He sat on a bench, watched the intricate water fountain at the center of the square. It was still early, but the commuters and businesspeople were already hurrying about on their way to jobs, juggling briefcases and coffees, babbling into cell phones and furiously texting on their BlackBerries. Not so long ago he'd been just like them, and now here he sat on a park bench like some loser. With a weary sigh, Jeff opened his newspaper to the *"Classified"* section.

He'd not been scanning the ads long when he noticed a strikingly attractive young woman scoping out the square. Dressed in a pinstripe skirt-suit and black heels, she stood out from the crowd and looked like an up-and-coming business executive, her raven-black hair styled perfectly, her makeup flawless. Sexy but professional, she held a leather briefcase in one hand and a cell phone to her ear with the other. She caught Jeff looking at her, smiled, then after saying something into the phone, slipped it into the side pocket of her briefcase and started toward him with a confident and purposeful stride.

Holy shit, she's coming over here. Heart racing, he quickly pretended to return his attention to the newspaper, but she'd already closed the gap between them. "Hey there," she said, her smoky voice laced with a slight raspy quality. "How are you?"

Jeff looked up over the paper as if he'd just noticed her. "Oh hi," he said, nervously clearing his throat. "I'm fine thanks. And you?"

"Outstanding." She bent her knees and placed the briefcase on the ground next to her, then reached inside the main compartment and removed a flyer of some sort.

Christ, he thought, *she's selling something.* Yet the woman looked far too well-dressed and successful to have a job peddling wares or handing out flyers to strangers on the street.

"I hope you won't think I'm being too forward, but may I ask a question?"

Jeff's cynical instincts kicked in but he still couldn't seem to get beyond how gorgeous the woman was. "Sure," he said, setting the newspaper aside, "ask away."

"Are you looking for work by any chance?"

"It's that obvious, huh?"

"Well, let's see. It's a little before nine in the morning on a weekday, you're sitting on a park bench rather than on your way to work, you're dressed casually—which means it's either your day off or you're unemployed—and you're reading…" With a mischievous glint in her eyes she looked to the bench and zeroed in on the newspaper, "…the classified section. Call me crazy, but I bet you're looking for a job."

"Impressive." *Did I just wink at her? I did. Jesus.* "Are you a detective?"

"Hardly."

"So I'm not under arrest then?"

This time she did the winking. "Not yet."

Gushing like a schoolboy, Jeff laughed longer and louder than seemed necessary. *Why am I so nervous? You'd think a beautiful woman had never spoken to me before. Eden's gorgeous, she—EDEN—shit, right, Eden. Ratchet it down a few million pegs before you get yourself in trouble, dipshit.*

"Check it out." She thrust the flyer at him, her bright smile still in place and her dark, exotic and catlike eyes studying him. "It could change your life."

Jeff took the flyer. It advertised interviews being conducted later that same day but gave no indication what the jobs were and no specific information about the company itself. IF YOU'RE SERIOUS ABOUT CHANGING YOUR LIFE WE MAY HAVE THE EMPLOYMENT OPPORTUNITY YOU'VE BEEN SEARCHING FOR. FOR ONE DAY AND ONE DAY ONLY, *INTERNATIONAL FACILITATOR, INC.* AND ITS CEO AND FOUNDER, WORLD-RENOWNED ENTREPRENUER F. HOPE, WILL BE CONDUCTING EXCLUSIVE INTERVIEWS IN YOUR CITY. IF YOU'RE RIGHT FOR US THIS COULD BE THE FIRST STEP TOWARD MAKING YOUR DREAMS COME TRUE.

He'd never heard of *International Facilitator, Inc.* or F. Hope, but whoever they were it was obviously some sort of con. Legitimate companies didn't recruit employees with street flyers. *Probably a sales seminar conducted by some douche bag with a middle-of-the-night infomercial,* Jeff thought. *A self-appointed expert sharing his 'secret' of success if you'll buy his insanely overpriced videos and books. Get in on it now and I'll make you rich. Uh-huh, sure you will.*

"It's not what you think," the woman assured him. He looked up at her questioningly.

"The expression on your face gave you away."

He attempted to hand the flyer back. "Thanks, I think I'm all set."

"I don't want to be a bother," she said, sliding onto the bench next to him. "But do you mind if I ask your name?"

Up close she was even more beautiful, and smelled intoxicating. He felt himself blush. "Jeff."

She extended her hand. It was dainty, with small, thin fingers, nails manicured, tapered and painted power red. "Jessica Bell."

He shook her hand. It was warm and soft and he felt a tingle that began in his lower back spread out across his entire body the moment they made contact. "Jeff," he said again, head spinning. "Jeff McGrath."

"It's a pleasure to meet you, Jeff."

"The pleasure's mine." He hoped to come off suave but knew he was more than likely making a fool of himself. He hadn't seriously flirted with anyone other than Eden in years and it showed.

"Frankly, Jeff," Jessica said in a conspiratorial tone, "I'd no longer have any interest in setting up an interview for you if you *weren't* skeptical. I know this whole thing seems suspect, but trust me, it's no scam. This is one of those instances in your life when you can either walk away or seize the moment, you know? A few years back, when one of his other recruiters approached me and handed me a flyer, I thought it was all a crock too. I was in New York, and I'd been working as a secretary at an accounting firm and taking acting classes at night. I wanted to be an actress back then, before Mr. Hope showed me my full potential. Anyway, I'd just been let go from the firm due to budget cuts and I was in trouble, a small town girl not long out of junior college and all alone in the big city, right? But I figured I had nothing to lose, so I went to the interview just for the hell of it. It changed my life, Jeff. It *changed* my life." Jessica crossed her legs then smoothed the skirt down over her knees. "You see, what I didn't know then was that the recruiters are trained to spot potential, to look for certain signs in individuals that indicate they might be right for our company. Back in New York the recruiter saw those signs in me. Just now, Jeff, I saw them in you."

Even though he knew it was probably all part of some carefully calculated pitch, he couldn't help but feel a bit flattered. Losing his job had damaged his self-esteem and confidence, and there were worse things than having a beautiful woman sit so close and say nice things about him.

"I'm curious," he said, "what exactly are those signs?"

"We're talking intangibles here."

"Can't even give me one example?"

She thought a moment before answering. "What I do involves instinct, utilizing a highly-developed ability to spot that special something in people that sets them apart. Strength, confidence—"

"And need?"

She relaxed her smile into something a bit more genuine. "And need," she confessed softly. "But if you'll notice, Jeff, this area is mobbed with people. The only person I've given a flyer to is you."

"Well, so far anyway."

"No. I was just about to leave when I spotted you sitting here." She drew a deep breath and let it out slowly, turning away from him and gazing out over the square. "Did you lose your job recently?"

"A few months back."

"Sales?"

"You're good."

"I'm well-trained. Were you in management?"

"Right again. Twelve years with the company, nine in management."

"What line?"

He arched an eyebrow. "I'm good, not psychic."

Jeff chuckled. "It was a high-end car audio business. We did sales and installation, but unfortunately the giant discount stores have wiped out most of the specialty chains."

"I noticed a wedding band. Do you have children too?"

Jeff relaxed a bit and decided to enjoy the game. "You tell me."

She turned back to him, looked deep into his eyes. "No kids."

"No." *Jesus,* he thought, *I'm actually swooning.* "Not yet anyway. Hopefully at some point soon but right now we're not in a position to—"

"Your wife works but doesn't make a whole lot, right? It's not enough, is it, Jeff? You're in financial trouble."

"It's getting tough, yes."

"Then tell me, what in the world do you have to lose at this point? There are a very limited number of slots, and I'll be honest, I only get paid if one of my finds actually gets hired. So if you're really not interested just tell me now, OK?"

"I thought I already had."

"OK," she said, hopping back to her feet, "it was nice to meet you then."

"Wait," he said. "How am I supposed to know if I'm interested when I don't have any particulars? I don't know what the job is or what your company does."

"It's a multifaceted company," she told him as she sank back down to the bench. "A great many tentacles, if you will, involved in a great many ventures. It's better to attend the interview and speak with Mr. Hope directly. He can give you the specifics and discuss things with you in detail. If I didn't think there was a position you'd be qualified for or worth training for, Jeff, I wouldn't be sitting here talking to you. Look at me, I was a secretary and was trained to be a recruiter, something I had no experience or even interest in until I was hired and saw the potential not only in the position, but in myself."

"Is this a company or a cult?"

"Oh, definitely a cult," she cracked. "But you don't get your official robe and hood until you eat your first baby under the light of a full moon."

Jeff couldn't take his eyes from her. "The interviews are today?"

"Yes, Mr. Hope will only be in Boston a few days. His time is limited."

"What the hell," he heard himself say, "I've got nothing else to do anyway."

"Awesome!"

"Where and when?"

She consulted her watch, which from the looks cost slightly more than his car. "The next available slot is around noon, 11:45, to be precise."

"Good, then I have time to run home, get into a suit and grab a resume."

"Not necessary. You're fine. Listen, have you had breakfast?"

"No, actually, I—"

"I'm starving." Jessica stood up, straightened her skirt and picked up her briefcase. "Want to join me for a bite to eat then we can head over to the interview? I'm staying over at the Plaza. They have a nice restaurant there. I hate eating alone, don't you?"

Jeff willed himself to remain seated. "I'm flattered, but my wife wouldn't—"

"It's OK, really." She smiled at him the way a child might smile at a puppy. "You love your wife and you don't fool around. I respect that, says a great deal about your character. But I was talking breakfast, not a weekend in Aruba. I'm thinking coffee, maybe a bagel and some conversation, nothing spectacular or adulterous. *Unless,*" she said, leaning closer, "sharing a pitcher of orange juice constitutes cheating, in which case we're into some seriously scandalous shit."

You ass, he thought. *She wasn't making a pass, she was just being nice. Or could be she's afraid if she let's me go now I'll blow off the interview later.*

"Come on, breakfast's on me." She offered him her free hand. "OK?"

Still mesmerized, Jeff placed his hand in hers. "OK."

3

Afterward, Jeff and Jessica took a cab to a small office building tucked away on an out-of-the-way side street in a drab neighborhood not far from the waterfront. They rode in awkward silence, Jessica fiddling with her cell phone—perhaps texting someone, he didn't look closely enough to know for sure—and Jeff trying desperately to remain calm and appease the tempest raging in his head. He'd no longer wanted to go to the interview, but had gone along anyway, allowing Jessica to lead him there as she might a pitiful, guilt-ridden dog on a leash. But all he could see, all he could think about, was Eden. And the very thought of her devastated him.

What have I done? Why did I—what have I done?

The building was old and dreary, just one in a line of several brownstones that had been converted into office space. Most looked unoccupied, and but for one burned-out carcass of an automobile near the end of the block, there were no parked cars or any signs of life whatsoever. Jeff took it all in, his depression and regret growing stronger with each passing second. *Just tell her you've changed your mind and you're no longer interested. Tell her you're going home.*

When the cab lurched to a stop Jessica put her phone away and turned to him, making eye contact for the first time since they'd left the hotel. "Ready?" Looking into her eyes he found it impossible to be angry with her or to feel anything but the primal attraction that had gotten him into this in the first place. He nodded submissively and forced a smile.

Once inside the unmarked building they arrived at a modest reception area, but the desk where a receptionist should've been sitting was empty. The office space was clearly a short-term rental, had a transient, unfinished feel and possessed no indicators that identified it as belonging to or being associated with any particular company or cause. Just beyond the reception area a row of plastic chairs sat in a line against the wall along a narrow hallway leading deeper into the building. Jessica told him to have a seat then slipped into the first office, closing the door behind her.

The building was eerily quiet, the usual din of city noises hushed here. Somewhere far off, the sound of a slowly dripping faucet echoed about with maddening repetition, but he couldn't quite hone in on its point of origin. At the very end of the hallway, in an open doorway which led to another part of the building he couldn't make out from there, Jeff noticed a man who looked to be in his late fifties or early sixties standing in the shadows. Was he waiting for an interview too, was he an employee, or was this F. Hope? Dressed in an inexpensive black suit, a white shirt and a skinny black tie, the man was unusually tall—probably close to seven feet—and thin to the point of appearing emaciated. He was bald with pointed features, his face long, drawn and skeletal.

Though he was a good thirty feet away, Jeff raised a hand, offered an apathetic wave and mumbled, "How's it going?"

He watched Jeff with the dark, sunken eyes of a man shackled with profound sorrow. His pale thin lips parted, as if he were about to respond, but then he seemed to think better of it, and with a slight nod of his head, turned and disappeared through the doorway.

What the hell am I doing here? Go—I—I should just go. Now, right now.

Jeff dropped his face into his hands and fought the desire to weep. He'd never felt so alone in his life. After a moment he looked up. There was no one else around, why not just get up and leave?

He was about to do just that when the office door opened and an elderly man poked his head out. "Mr. McGrath?"

"Yes."

"Please." The man stepped back and opened wide the door.

He was dressed in a cream-colored summer suit, his snow-white hair neatly combed into place, straight back and away from a face with badly aged features. Jeff guessed that in the man's youth those same features had been chiseled, and he'd probably been quite handsome. "Won't you come in?"

On shaky legs, Jeff entered the windowless office. Sparsely furnished, with only a meeting table and two plastic chairs, there was a box of donuts, a coffeemaker and a stack of Styrofoam cups at one end, and a clipboard with a standard employment application at the other. On the far wall, another door through which Jessica had apparently gone prior to his arrival stood closed.

"Hope," the man said, offering his hand, "Foster Hope."

"Jeff McGrath." As they shook hands Jeff was struck by how clammy Hope's palm was. *Like shaking hands with a corpse,* he thought. *And is he kidding with that name?*

"Since I'm sure you're wondering," he said with a wry smile, "yes, that is my real name. You don't honestly think I'd make up such a thing, do you?"

"No, sir," he answered, attempting a smile of his own.

Hope released his hand and motioned to one of the chairs. "Take a seat."

Jeff slid into the chair closest to the door as the old man sat in the other. Hope shifted his position so he was facing Jeff. With a small frame and pale complexion, he was rather unremarkable, except for a pair of piercing green eyes that were so bright they looked artificial. Jeff figured them for contact lenses.

"So you're looking for work."

It wasn't a question but he answered it anyway. "I am."

"Hardly uncommon these days, I'm sorry to say."

"Rough economy right now," Jeff agreed, "lots of people out of work."

"I'm actually semi-retired," the old man said. "As luck would have it I did quite well for myself, but my time's passing. There comes a day in everyone's life when it's time to step aside for the next generation of go-getters."

"Plenty of go-getters," Jeff said, "just not enough jobs."

"Of course it was a different time when I was coming up. I went to war when I was young, but once it was over and I came home my father built a house for my new family and me and we settled in nicely. Things were different then, easier, not so complicated as the world's become since. At any rate, he was quite talented in that regard, my father, one of those men with a natural gift for building things, you know the type. I always envied him that, as I had absolutely no skill in those areas whatsoever. I'd always been a good talker, though, had the gift of gab as they say, and I'm a good negotiator, so I became a salesman. Ms. Bell told me you're in sales too."

The very mention of Jessica brought visions of Eden crashing down on him again. Guilt struck him like a baseball bat to the back of the head.

"Well at least up until a few months ago, eh?" Hope smiled as if pleased. "Car audio, wasn't it?"

Jeff nodded.

"Are you feeling all right?" Mr. Hope adjusted his already perfectly positioned necktie. "You look a tad *peaked*."

"I apologize. I'm just tired, haven't been sleeping particularly well." Jeff cleared his throat and sat up straighter in the chair. "So what exactly does your company sell?"

"Oh, I've been in sales for years now, little of this, little of that, but a long while ago I found my niche in insurance."

Inwardly, Jeff cringed. In sales circles the only thing worse than selling cars was selling insurance. It was the end of the road for most salespeople, and unless you were exceptionally good at it and more than a little lucky, insurance was one tough way to earn a living. "I don't mean to be rude, but if it's a position in insurance sales you're offering, I—"

"I don't recall *offering* anything."

Jeff drew a deep breath. "I understand. I'm just not interested in—"

"Tell me about your last job." The old man put an elbow on the table and let his chin rest in his hand, those severe green eyes glittering like emeralds.

"I worked for a company over on Tremont Street," Jeff explained. "Unfortunately the big discount chains made it impossible for us to stay in business. Twelve years and just like that I'm out on the street."

"Dreadful," Hope sighed, "positively dreadful. Do you have a family?"

"I'm married but we don't have children."

"Does your wife work?"

"She's a receptionist."

"At least you've got her income." He seemed more upset with the situation than Jeff was. "It's unforgivable the way companies treat people nowadays. Shameful, particularly in this economy, or lack thereof, I should say."

"Well, I like to think that any good salesman isn't unemployed long."

"That's a sound philosophy, young man." Hope looked away a moment, as if he'd slipped into deep thought. "I understand you're not interested in selling insurance, and while that is part of what we do here at *International Facilitator, Inc.*, it's only the tip of the proverbial iceberg. We sell many things and offer many services. Tell me Jeff, do you have your heart set on a sales position, or might you be interested in a slightly different line of work?"

"Sales and sales management are the only things I've ever done."

"Then maybe it's time to try something new."

"Maybe it is."

"Remember the old tale about the man that discovers a genie in a bottle, frees him, and is granted three wishes?" He smiled warmly, revealing a large set of chalk-white teeth that were obviously dentures. "Have you ever thought about the wishes you'd make if you were that man?"

Oh spare me, Jeff thought, *here comes one of those lame scenario deals where he makes a point, shows you how clever he is then thinks your answers will actually give him some deep insight into who you are.* "Not really, no."

Mr. Hope slowly blinked his eyes. "I know it sounds silly, but it's actually a good way to gage a person. One's answers tend to reveal an awful lot about the individual."

Fine, just play along. "Makes sense."

"If you could have only one wish, Jeff, what would it be?"

"You mean besides world peace?"

His answer seemed to amuse the old man. "Yes, besides that."

"I'd like to be financially independent."

"Go on."

"If I never had to worry about covering the rent or credit card bills, car payments—all of it—if I could live without having to worry about all that stuff and just be financially independent, I'd be the happiest man in the world."

"You want to be rich then?"

"That'd be nice, but I'd be happy just being comfortable enough to be able to pay our bills and live life without constantly having to worry about money."

"And what would you say if I told you I could grant such a wish?"

"Let me guess. You're a genie."

"Wouldn't *that* be something?" The old man laughed heartily and waved a liver-spotted hand in the air. "No, no, I'm just a businessman, Jeff. Although, at the risk of sounding rather crude, a very successful, wealthy businessman."

"Well you certainly have my attention, sir."

"Good, because the position I think might be right for you pays quite well. If you're able to perform your job successfully, it could easily yield a level of compensation that would make your wish for financial independence a reality. So as you can imagine, we don't just interview anyone for this kind of position. It takes someone special. Are you special, Jeff?"

"I'd like to think so."

"You seem like a nice young man, a bright, articulate, hardworking and conscientious fellow, someone who could not only use a break, but someone who deserves one."

"Thank you, I appreciate that."

"Jeff, I've spent my life reading people. In sales you have to immediately discern a person's strengths and weaknesses, you know that yourself. The best salespeople are excellent judges of character, and use that to their advantage. I've been around a long time. I know a good man when I see one. You're just down on your luck, that's all."

Jeff crossed his legs and attempted a relaxed posture. "So what kind of position are we talking about then?"

"Specifically, I have an opening for a negotiator. My company employs several to handle negotiations with clients when it becomes necessary or when it's beneficial for us or both parties. I've found those with sales backgrounds tend to be perfect for the positions."

"I see," Jeff said, though he had no idea what he was talking about. "So, negotiations as in..."

There was a soft but sudden knock on the interior door. As Mr. Hope turned in its direction, it opened and a mousy middle-aged woman in a frumpy dress leaned into the room, her brown eyes comically large due to a pair of eyeglasses with black plastic frames and unusually thick lenses. "I'm sorry to interrupt, sir, but you have an extremely important phone call."

"Thank you, Ms. Gill. Tell whoever it is I'll be with them momentarily." He struggled to his feet with a weary sigh as the woman retreated, closing the door behind her. "Jeff, go ahead and fill out an application." He slid the clipboard over to him. "It's just a formality, really, but a necessary one. I won't be long. This shouldn't take but a minute or two. And help yourself to a cup of coffee, perhaps a donut."

Once Hope had left the room, Jeff took a look at the application. It was generic and unimaginative and requested little beyond the basics: full name, address, social security number, phone number, education and work history and two lines for references, one personal, one professional. He considered the application a moment, unsure if he wanted to continue. *You've come this far, he thought. Might as well stick it out and see what happens. What happened earlier is over and done with, and nothing can ever change that now.* He sighed, ran a hand over his face and back through his hair then picked up the pen lying next to the clipboard. A new and lucrative career could solve all their problems. *You've done some stupid-ass shit in your life, but you really stepped in it this time, boy. You fucked up, and huge, but this might be a way to do something right. If this job pays as well as Hope says it does and you get it, you could go to Eden with some good news for a change. Clear your head and get in the game, moron, this could be your one chance to really come through for you and your wife. And you owe her, you piece of shit.*

Jeff poured himself a cup of coffee then filled out the application.

While awaiting Mr. Hope's return, he heard strange shuffling sounds in the hallway behind him, and then muffled voices beyond the door on the back wall. Jeff couldn't be certain but one of the voices sounded like Hope. The tone indicated he was reprimanding someone, though it was hard to tell for sure. Not long afterward, Foster Hope returned to the room, closed the door and sat in the chair he'd occupied earlier. "I apologize for the interruption. I'm sure you understand these things are often unavoidable."

"Perfectly understandable, sir," Jeff said, game face firmly in place.

"Where were we?"

"We were about to discuss specifics regarding the negotiator position."

"Of course." He crossed his legs and assumed a more relaxed posture. "I'm from the old school—call me foolish if you will—but I've never believed in the need for formal written contracts unless it's absolutely necessary to protect both parties. In my day, for the most part, a person's word was sufficient. And do you know why, Jeff? Because in my day one's word had significance and meaning, it meant something beyond words or even intentions. It had weight, do you understand?"

"I do."

He gave a sheepish shrug. "At any rate, due to the way in which I sometimes conduct business, it becomes necessary for one of my negotiators to convince clients that they need to do the right thing. Settle their accounts, fulfill whatever they agreed to in a given business deal, etc. Most of the time it's a simple oversight or miscommunication, but now and then people actually try to double-cross us. Regardless, these matters must be attended to and resolved, and that's where the company negotiators come in."

"Isn't that why God created lawyers?"

"I promise you, God had nothing to do with the creation of lawyers." Hope chuckled softly. "No, these situations are delicate and need to be handled with the utmost care, professionalism and above all, discretion. Those who can perform these duties well are not easy to find, Jeff, so when we come across someone we feel is right for the job we pay them handsomely."

That's the deal then, this is some sort of criminal enterprise, Jeff thought. *I should've known this was all too good to be true.* "With all due respect Mr. Hope, I'm a salesman, not a leg-breaker. If you want to hire a goon to lean on people there are plenty of characters in the city that do that kind of thing. I'm just not one of them."

"No, you misunderstand, that's not what I'm looking for at all. I *abhor* violence, even the mere threat of it. I've seen violence, real violence, and there's nothing glamorous or appealing about it, trust me. Anyone that's ever traversed a battlefield will tell you the same thing. I simply need someone to calmly and rationally convince delinquent clients that it's in everyone's best interest if they do the right thing. It's a negotiation, not a threat or intimidation. Who better than a gifted salesman like yourself to talk to someone and sell them, in a sense, on the appropriate course of action? Besides, the kind of scum you're referring to are wholly unnecessary in these situations. It's been a personal policy of mine for years to never deal or interact in any way with those sorts of individuals. Frankly, they scare me. I'm a legitimate businessman, Jeff, not a criminal." Mr. Hope scratched at his cheek delicately and smiled. "I need people I can trust, people with ethics and morals, businesspeople, professionals. I need someone who can do this job correctly, in a civil manner, and if that someone has a particular need that I'm in a position to meet by hiring them in exchange for their services, all the better. Of course even if we did decide to offer you the position, were you to find it unsuitable, simply resign and we'll part as friends. But hopefully you'd find it to your liking, remain with us and excel in the position. However you must also understand that you'd begin on a trial basis. Generally the period only lasts the length of a single assignment, and we make a decision from there whether it's working for us or not. Again, if not, we part as friends. But if we like what we see once you're in action then we move forward together and welcome you permanently to the *International Facilitator* family."

Though Hope's explanation helped to soften his initial apprehension, he wasn't sure he liked the emphasis the old man put on the word *permanently*. It was an odd conversation at best, and with a total stranger to boot, but curiosity had slowly gotten the better of him. He still knew virtually nothing in terms of specifics, but that would come later. He needed this job and the hefty salary promised along with it. "Well I hope we can pursue this then," he said. "I think I'd like to learn more and see where it takes me."

"Splendid." Hope rose to his feet and gave Jeff a pat on the shoulder. "We'll review your application information and someone will be back to you very shortly, most likely later this evening or perhaps tomorrow. If you haven't heard from us by tomorrow evening you can assume we've decided to go in a different direction. I thank you for your time."

"Not at all, thank *you*, sir." Jeff stood and they shook hands. "I look forward to hearing from you."

"I take it you can see yourself out. Good day."

Jeff watched the old man turn and stride off through the door, uncertain if this was the luckiest day of his life, a total waste of a few hours, or if he'd just met the Devil himself.

4

When Jeff returned to his apartment building he saw that the homeless man had again taken up position on the front steps. Though it annoyed him he was too distracted by everything that had taken place that morning to give a damn. Rather than confront him he simply flashed the man a dirty look then started up the stairs without comment.

"You should stay away from her."

Jeff froze, slowly turned back to him. "Excuse me?"

"The woman you were talking to before." The man looked up at him. "You should stay away from her."

Anger welled in him, followed by a touch of fear. "What woman?"

"The pretty one you were talking to in Copley Square."

"I don't know what you're talking about."

"Yes you do."

"Have you been following me?"

The man shook his head and sighed.

"Answer me," Jeff said, moving a step closer.

"No," he mumbled, "I haven't been following you."

"Then how do you know about her?"

"I was already hanging at Copley Square. A vendor there gives me a pretzel for free every morning. He's a good guy. Anyway, I saw you talking to that woman. Then I saw you two leave together."

"Yeah, well that's none of your business."

"She offered you work, didn't she?"

Jeff tried to swallow, nearly choked. "How do you know that?"

"Guy like me, I see a lot, hear a lot. Most folk—especially city folk—don't notice someone like me. No more than streetlights, garbage cans or telephone wires running over their heads. It's all right there in front of them, but they learn to filter it out until they don't even see it anymore."

"Apparently you missed your calling as a poet, but—"

"I'm just saying you should stay away from her is all."

"And why would you say that? Do you even know who she is?"

"Do *you*?"

"It was a business meeting and none of your concern, I—for Christ's sake—I don't have to stand out here and explain myself to some homeless loser like you." Jeff stabbed a finger at him. "You stay the hell away from—"

"I'm trying to help you."

"Well if you don't mind I'll skip the life advice from the local neighborhood bum." Jeff started up the steps again then thought better of it and turned back. "I'm not telling you again. Stay away from me, my wife and this building. Got it?"

"I'm not some piece of garbage, you know," the man said, his face a mask of sorrow. "I'm a human being, the same as you."

"You're nothing like me."

"Neither is your wife. She's a very nice person."

"Leave my wife out of this."

The man struggled to his feet and stumbled back a few steps, bloodshot eyes never leaving Jeff. "She's beautiful, intelligent, caring and *very* giving."

"Get the fuck out of here or I'll call the cops."

"Do you ever wonder what she sees in you?"

"I'm warning you, asshole." Jeff's hands clenched to fists. "Stay away."

"Or what?"

"Or I'll kill you."

"Go ahead." The man smiled. His teeth were brown, many were broken, his gums bloody and diseased. "I'm dying anyway."

Jeff was still taking the stairs to his apartment when his cell phone began to ring. His former coworker Craig Henderson's number appeared on the small screen. They'd worked together for years and Craig had become his closest friend in that time. "Hey, man." Jeff pinned the phone between shoulder and cheek as he fumbled keys from his coat pocket. "What's up?"

"Got some great news."

"Good, I could use some."

"You know that general manager gig I was going for at that independent superstore on the cape? They just called me back. I got it."

Jeff unlocked the apartment, slipped inside, closed the door and leaned back against it. "Congratulations, Craig, that's awesome."

"Here's where you come in. I can replace any existing staff I want. If you're up for running the car audio department I'll bounce the current guy."

The idea that someone else would have to lose their job in order for him to get one was troubling, but Jeff told himself he couldn't worry about such things. "It's a bit of a commute but yeah, of course, definitely."

"Not exactly sure what the salary is because I haven't seen the budget yet, but from the numbers they threw at me I know it'll be real close to what you were making before. I start next week. You'd be starting about a week later."

"Sounds good." He pushed away from the door and tossed his keys on the kitchen counter. "I'll take it."

"Then consider yourself hired, bro. I'll be back to you in a day or two, soon as I know the particulars. I'm taking Katy and the kids out to dinner tonight, the drought is officially over!"

"Craig, seriously, man, thank you. You just saved my ass."

"You'd do the same for me. Talk to you soon."

"Later." Jeff disconnected then forced himself to stand still a moment and take it all in. The guilt about what had taken place earlier continued to throttle him relentlessly, but for the moment it took a backseat to relief and joy. He knew it would be a long time—if ever—before he'd be able to forgive himself for what he'd done, but at least at this point the job would allow him to get them out of debt and back on the right track. It also meant he could forget about Jessica Bell, Foster Hope and whatever the hell their creepy company was all about.

From now on, I'll make it right. I'll do everything in my power to make Eden the happiest woman on the face of the Earth. I'll never screw up like this again.

With newfound purpose, Jeff showered, changed his clothes then headed out to the local market. Without care for what things cost, he filled a shopping cart and got all the items he'd need to put together a romantic dinner at home. He'd get the apartment cleaned, make a nice meal, maybe light a few candles and then, over a glass of wine, break the good news to Eden.

He had just unloaded all the groceries when a call came into the house phone. "Hello?"

"Jeff?"

He recognized the voice immediately but pretended he hadn't. "Yes?"

"Jessica Bell."

"Hi."

"Hi. I wanted to let you know we've reviewed your application and everything seems to be in order. Mr. Hope has given me the authority to go ahead and offer you the position. He'll discuss salary and benefits with you himself. He'd like you to come into the offices where you interviewed tomorrow morning for an orientation and—"

"Jessica, I'm sorry to interrupt, and please tell Mr. Hope I appreciate the offer, but I've actually taken another position."

"I see."

"But again, thanks for your time and—"

"Jeff, this is *very* disappointing."

"I'm sorry, but as I say, I've already accepted another position."

"I hope this isn't about what happened between us."

He pinched the bridge of his nose, hoping to head off the headache that was drifting in behind his eyes. "That was a mistake," he said softly. "I'm not upset with you, I—it's not like we planned it, we—it just happened and I feel terrible about the whole thing. Look, I'd rather not discuss it, OK? I have to go."

"So there's nothing I can do to persuade you to—"

"No, there isn't."

"Mr. Hope will not be pleased."

"I apologize if I wasted your time or his, but—"

"Did you hear what I said? Mr. Hope will *not* be pleased."

OK, enough. "Well that's too bad, Jessica, but not my problem."

"Are you sure?"

"What's that supposed to mean?" He shuddered from a sudden chill as a quick burst of nervous laughter escaped him. "Are you *threatening* me?"

"I'll let Mr. Hope know of your decision. Good luck to you."

Though the line clicked and fell silent with disturbing finality, Jeff couldn't shake the feeling that he hadn't heard the last of these people.

5

Eden entered the apartment looking haggard and exhausted, purse slung over her shoulder, a plastic bag containing items she purchased from the local drugstore in one hand and her keys in the other. Just inside the door, she hesitated and looked to the table. It was set with their good china and silver, their best cloth napkins and draped with a matching tablecloth. Red candles burned in silver holders on either side of a beautiful flower centerpiece, and the aroma of broiled steaks and a hint of garlic filled the air. She smiled cautiously as she dropped her purse on the counter and crept deeper into the room.

"Jeff?"

He stepped in from the kitchen wearing an apron, a large serving spoon in hand. "Good evening," he said through a wide smile.

"What's all this?"

"I'm making us dinner, steaks—and not just any steaks but top of the line Porterhouses—angel hair pasta with shrimp in butter and garlic sauce, and a freshly-tossed garden salad. I also grabbed a bottle of really good wine, so why don't you go get changed into something comfortable and I'll pour you a glass?"

"Jeff—"

"Dinner should be ready in about fifteen minutes." She slumped against the counter, deflated.

"Sweetie, are you out of your mind? We can't afford all this."

"Oh, but we can." He grinned.

She watched him a moment, waiting. "We can?"

"Remember the job down the cape Craig was up for? He got it."

"OK. And..."

"He called this afternoon and offered me a position managing the car audio department. I start in two weeks. Don't have an exact figure on the salary yet but he said it'd be in the same ballpark as what I was making before."

Eden stared at him as if he'd spoken Swahili. "Well don't just stand there looking all gorgeous," he said, playfully pointing the spoon at her. "Go get changed. Let's celebrate."

Without a word she vaulted across the space separating them and threw her arms around his neck with such force they nearly collapsed. Laughing, Jeff held her in his arms as she peppered his face and neck with kisses. "Oh Jeff," she said breathlessly, "I'm so happy, I—are you happy?—we were in so much trouble, you have no idea how bad—this is great!"

"We're going to be just fine," he told her, his free hand gently stroking her cheek. Feeling her so close to him and so happy filled him with a rush of joy he hadn't experienced in months, but it made the guilt stronger, too. She was so beautiful, so unaware, so completely trusting. How could he have betrayed her?

Before he could think anymore about it, Eden kissed him again. One kiss became two, and two became three, and finally, as they kissed passionately she dragged him back across the room until they had both fallen onto the couch, laughing and tickling each other.

"Dinner!" he reminded her.

As they settled down, him atop her, she gazed lovingly into his eyes and held him close. "Let it burn."

Later that night rain fell over the city but did little to combat the oppressive heat. Jeff drifted off to sleep listening to its steady cadence, oddly aware that the sound was shifting, changing and slowly becoming something else...the faint rhythm of ancient Arabic music echoing in his ears, the ethereal cries of exotic flutes and various percussion instruments dancing and swaying about him like whispered remnants from some distant time. And then from the darkness came blinding light. Stretched out before him was an open expanse of desert for far as the eye could see; the sand so pale it was nearly white. Shuffling beneath a blistering sun, Jeff trudged up the side of an enormous dune. As he reached the summit he saw a lone tree in the valley between this and the next dune. Large and peculiarly jutting up out of the sand, the tree's branches were long-dead, gnarled and reached toward an unforgiving sky. Lying at its base was a leopard, its deep golden color and spotted coat contrasting sharply against the white sand. As the music grew louder and more intoxicating, a woman emerged through the waves of heat rising from the desert floor as if she'd been burned into existence just then by the relentless sun.

Nude and glistening with sweat, Jessica, curled up next to the beast, her hair a wild and tangled rat's nest, eyes wide and smeared with swathes of thick black makeup, lips painted blood-red. Her hands slid back and forth with erotic precision along the leopard's flank.

Jeff froze, heart racing. The leopard blinked slowly, watching him with regal indifference as a low growl emanated forth, majestic and violent.

The distant horizon began to shift and change, growing darker then darker still as the beginnings of a storm roiled and surged across the desert, kicking up great black clouds as if summoned straight from the bowels of Hell.

And somewhere in the turmoil, he heard Jessica laughing seductively.

The sound of voices woke him, luring him from sleep gradually. As Jeff drifted closer to consciousness he realized he was not in a desert but the relative safety of his own bed. Still, he was certain he'd heard voices. The bedroom windows were open, perhaps the intrusion had come from outside and could be blamed on inconsiderate passersby having a latenight conversation.

Still trying to sort out the thoughts filling his head, he reached for Eden. She was next to him, nude and asleep on her stomach, her back rising and falling in a slow and steady rhythm, bare skin damp with perspiration.

The apartment still smelled vaguely of dinner, and as the strange visions from his dream faded, Jeff felt himself smile.

Draping an arm across his forehead, he watched the darkness move gracefully, like water stirred by a gentle breeze. It seemed almost…*alive.*

He listened a moment. The voices had stopped.

Maybe I was still dreaming when I heard them.

Jeff closed his eyes and zeroed in on the downpour a while.

Through the soft hissing rain the voices returned, this time sounding like they'd been whispered from somewhere *inside* the apartment. He opened his eyes and looked to the door. It was open. He brought his hand down to his face, rubbed his eyes and fought a losing battle to suppress a yawn. Once it passed, he drew quiet, shallow breaths and strained to listen. Nothing…

His head tingled, and the sensation quickly moved through him, as if his entire body had fallen asleep. Jeff blinked a few times and ran a hand over his chest. Like Eden, he was damp with perspiration. He wiped his palm on the sheet and struggled up onto his elbows, propping himself into a semi-sitting position and focusing his vision as best he could.

Something shifted, separated from the darkness… something in the doorway. Or was it the door itself? Was it moving…*closing*?

Jeff squinted into the darkness. *My glasses…*

He knew they were on the nightstand where he'd left them, and his mind told him to reach over, pick them up then switch on the nightstand lamp, to call out and warn Eden that there was an intruder in the room, to jump from bed and confront whoever had broken into the apartment. But he couldn't move. He tried to scream, but could only manage a choking sound.

The door swung partially closed, enough to reveal that someone had been standing behind it all along. An indistinct silhouette crept across the wall…

Foster Hope stood mere feet from the bed, glaring at him excitedly with the same yellow eyes the leopard had possessed in Jeff's dream. But before he could fully comprehend what he was seeing, the old man's eyes turned black and cold and his lips quivered into a hideously demonic grin. A tongue, impossibly long and black, darted from his mouth like a snake, slithering about as if for purchase.

I'm dreaming, I—this is a nightmare, just a nightmare—I'm dreaming.

Hope's liver-spotted hands reached out through the shadows, the fingernails long and curved, shiny white talons of bone piercing darkness.

The razor-sharp tips dripped what could only be blood, and it wasn't until he moved even closer that Jeff realized Hope, like them, was completely nude. But something had wrapped itself around the lower portion of the old man's body and was clinging to his pallid legs. Something alive and moist, coiled about his knees and thighs, writhing and pulsing like some slimy creature, perhaps a skinned human appendage or a thick serpent-like entity with a network of spiderweb veins traversing a mass the color of raw meat.

Hopelessly paralyzed, Jeff watched with horror as the man glided toward the side of the bed. Eden's side. Struggling, Jeff tried to scream, but his throat constricted and felt as if someone was strangling him. Though he couldn't see them, he felt the unmistakable grip of cold ghostly hands wrap around his throat and tighten like a vise. Familiar hands…feminine hands…

Others had joined them. But were they…*people*? They moved swiftly beneath the cover of shadow, hurrying about beyond the bedroom doorway and throughout the apartment.

This is a dream, a—a nightmare—

"There are no nightmares," the old man said, flickering tongue slurring his speech. "There is only the torment of darkness."

Eyes wide, Jeff's body bucked and convulsed against strangulation as spittle bubbled in a thick froth from his mouth.

The bed shifted. Small shadowy forms scurried up over the foot of the bed, growling and clawing at the lone sheet until it fell away and Foster Hope reached for Eden's exposed flesh.

Deep guttural laughter filled the room, and Jeff's mind splintered as he spiraled down into a boundless darkness the likes of which he'd never before experienced.

Madness, it seemed, had swallowed him whole.

6

Though he'd been more or less awake for several minutes, Jeff remained in bed, flat on his back, the sheet tangled around him like a toga. Despite the early hour the humidity was already high and hung over the room like a shroud. He couldn't remember the last time he'd slept so late. Sluggishly, he studied a series of hairline cracks in the bedroom ceiling a while. Distanced from his nightmares, they no longer held much power over him, but their memory remained vivid in his mind. Remnants of a headache scraped at his temples then faded as he turned his attention to the gliding motion of an oscillating fan on the bureau.

The sound of Eden's heels clacking against the floor preceded her, and as she swept into the room with an enthusiasm and glee she hadn't shown in a very long time, Jeff caught a whiff of her cologne. It was quickly dissipated by the fan. Makeup done and hair styled, she was dressed in a skirt and blouse and ready for work. "It's alive!" she chuckled. "You were out cold and snoring so loud at one point the whole room was shaking."

"A little too much wine, I guess."

"You were having bad dreams too, you kept moaning in your sleep."

"Yeah, had some strange ones last night." He sat up and swung his legs around to the floor. "What time is it?"

"Little after eight."

He rubbed the back of his neck with one hand and snatched his glasses from the nightstand with the other. "Can't remember the last time I slept this late."

"Enjoy it while you can, you'll be back in the rat race soon."

She leaned close, and they kissed. "Gotta run."

Jeff slid his glasses on. "See you tonight. Have a good day, baby."

"Love you."

"I love you, too."

She stopped at the door and looked back at him. "Jeff, I…I'm sorry things have been so tense these last few months."

"Me too. But it's over now, OK?"

Her smile lit up the room. "OK."

"Everything's going to be fine from here on out. I promise."

After Eden left for work, Jeff had a bowl of cereal, watched CNN for a bit then showered, shaved and threw on a pair of jeans, a T-shirt and sneakers. He was about to give Craig a call when the buzzer rang.

He looked out the window at the front steps and saw a young guy in spandex and a helmet holding a large manila envelope in hand, his bicycle chained to a streetlight a few feet away. Jeff raised the screen, poked his head out and called down to him. "Can I help you?"

The man looked up. "Oh. Hey. Courier service. Got a delivery for…" He glanced at the envelope.

"Jeff McGrath."

"That's me. I'll buzz you up."

A few moments later he opened the apartment door to find the lanky, heavily tattooed courier had just made it to the landing. He was drenched in sweat and looked like he hadn't bathed or laundered his outfit in several days. When he got closer the smell confirmed it. "This heat's a bitch," he said with the detached boredom of a teenager. "Just won't let up."

"Yeah, hopefully it'll break soon, huh?" With a nod, he handed Jeff the envelope.

Something about the kid's eyes didn't seem quite right. Was he stoned?

"Problem?" the courier sighed.

"No, I—sorry—do I have to sign or anything?"

A mocking smile spread slowly across the courier's face as he pulled a bottle of water from his belt and started back down the stairs. "All set."

"Thanks." Jeff closed the door. *Something creepy about that kid,* he thought. But he dismissed it and quickly returned his attention to the envelope. It felt nearly weightless. His name had been written across the front in magic marker but there was no return address or anything that suggested where the envelope originated from.

He tore the top open. A silver disc slid out.

The label designated it a DVD-R and revealed the manufacturer's name but offered nothing else. Confused and more than a little nervous, Jeff forced himself to the entertainment center on the far wall, turned on the television then slid the disc into the DVD player. Remote in hand, he backed away to the couch and hit PLAY. Static filled the screen. Jeff was about to hit fast-forward when the screen blinked and the snow was replaced with darkness. An eerie and monotonous rumbling sound groaned through the speakers like the drone of some unknown machinery. A few bars of interference bent and rippled across the black screen, and then slowly, the darkness gave way to reveal grainy black-and-white footage shot by what appeared to be an old VHS camcorder of some sort. The frame blinked and became a hotel room.

Jeff's hands began to shake. He wanted to hit the STOP button on the remote but his finger refused to cooperate. Throat dry and eyes watering with fear and rage, he watched as he and Jessica entered the room. They'd had breakfast, and after an hour of flirting, she'd insisted he come with her up to the room for a minute, using the excuse that she needed to get something for his interview before they left. He'd agreed, already knowing what was about to happen. And now he watched himself nervously fidgeting just inside the hotel room door as Jessica reached around him, purposely crushing her breasts against his chest as she hung a DO NOT DISTURB sign on the knob.

There was still no audio, only the continuous rumbling sound.

He watched as Jessica pulled the door closed, their faces nearly touching. And then they were kissing, their bodies suddenly entangled.

Jeff's legs wobbled and he sank down onto the couch, remote

still aimed at the television. He looked closer. Apparently the person filming had been on the far side of the room, near the bathroom, but how had he not seen him standing there? He and Jessica fell back onto the bed, him atop her. Free hand to his mouth, Jeff tried to breathe, watching as the camera moved closer. But he could tell from the motion that the operator hadn't zoomed in, he'd actually stepped closer. So close in fact, that he was only a few feet away, standing right next to the bed where he and Jessica were rolling about, pulling at each other's clothes.

It's impossible, I—I would've seen the person standing there, I…

Slowly, the camera turned back toward the person using it.

An unsettling gaunt face filled the frame. Jeff recognized him as the tall thin man he'd briefly seen in the hallway of the building where Foster Hope had interviewed him. The man's bald head, long face, emaciated and skeletal, tilted slowly to the right, dark sunken eyes staring at him as if he could see Jeff sitting there watching at that very moment, pale thin lips drawn into a horrifying grimace equal parts misery and cruelty.

The camera turned again, panned across the bed long enough to clearly show Jeff and Jessica nude and making love, and then continued on to the opposite corner of the room.

Someone else was there, standing in the shadows just beyond the nightstand. A liver-spotted hand reached through the dim light to a telephone there, lifted the handset then punched in a series of numbers.

The screen blinked, went blank for a split-second then came back into focus. This time it was aimed at the outside of Jeff's apartment building and appeared to have been shot very late at night. The droning sound continued, became slightly louder and then the image turned back to snow.

Jeff sat staring at the TV until the snow switched to a blank screen, indicating the material on the disc had ended.

Shaken, Jeff rose from the couch, switched the television off and ejected the disc. He was still holding and staring at it numbly when the phone rang.

Without speaking, he raised the phone to his ear. "Hello Jeff."

A chill ran up his back.

"You can't possibly be surprised to hear from me," Hope

said. "You just saw me dialing didn't you? Who did you think I was calling?"

"What are you doing, I—what's this all about?" Jeff squeezed his eyes shut in an attempt to stop the room from spinning. "Who are you people?"

"It's not as if we haven't already met, Jeff." The old man sighed into the phone, but it was forced, phony. "Of course I was very disappointed to hear you'd turned down my generous job offer. I thought perhaps I could persuade you to reconsider. Before you answer, you should know that as we speak, another copy of the disc is on its way to your wife's workplace. It should be delivered to her any moment now. Should you change your mind and choose to come to work for me I could easily stop the delivery, but there isn't much time, I'm afraid, so I'll need your decision as quickly as possible."

Jeff ran a hand through his hair and began pacing the room like a caged animal. "Why are you doing this?"

"What am I doing?"

"You know goddamn well what you're doing. You're blackmailing me!"

"Oh how distasteful, I'm doing no such thing. No one has forced you to do anything, and no one ever will. You've simply made choices, Jeff, decisions. You've made them on your own. No one forced you to speak to Ms. Bell. No one forced you to accompany her back to her hotel. No one forced you to have breakfast with her. No one forced you to sleep with her. No one forced you to come and interview with me. And no one is forcing you to do anything now. I'm presenting you with options. This decision, like all the others before and after it, is yours and yours alone."

"I haven't done anything to you, I—we don't even know each other—why would you do this to me? It's been a setup from the start, but *why*? What do I possibly have you could want? I'm broke, I don't have any money."

Hope breathed heavily into the phone, Jeff's torment clearly exciting him. "We don't have much time, Jeff. Should I have the delivery canceled? Or would you rather take your chances and allow your wife to see the disc?"

Jeff gripped the phone so tightly it hurt his hand. "No… don't…"

"Don't?"

"Keep Eden out of this. Cancel the delivery, I—I'll do whatever you want."

"Consider it done, Jeff." A muffled sound as he covered the phone with his hand, and then: "Now, I believe you and I have an appointment, yes?"

"Yes."

"You know where to find me," Hope said evenly. "I'll be waiting."

The line clicked, died.

And in that moment, in many ways, so did Jeff McGrath.

7

Still badly shaken, Jeff fired up their computer and plugged both *Foster Hope* and *International Facilitator, Inc.* into numerous search engines. They returned no information on either. *Foster Hope* simply resulted in several plays on the words and websites for various charities in which the word 'hope' was used in their name or information. *International Facilitator, Inc.* led to several management consulting firms, international businesses and the like, but nothing by that name and nothing that indicated the company even existed. He next tried *Jessica Bell,* but because it was such a common name it returned literally hundreds of hits. He checked several, but none were her.

After walking the apartment, replaying everything in his mind and trying to figure out what to do, Jeff finally decided to go see Craig first. He obviously had no choice but to keep his appointment with Foster Hope, or another disc would certainly be delivered to Eden before the day was through, but he and Craig had been friends a long time and Jeff knew he could confide in him. Maybe he'd know what to do. A clear-headed, objective opinion of everything that was taking place was needed, and Craig could provide him with that.

Disc in hand, he hurried down the stairs and out the building. He looked around for the homeless man but he was nowhere to be found. His cryptic warning still lingered in Jeff's mind, only now it had taken on even greater sinister meaning. *You should stay away from her.* "The one fucking time I want him to be here," he mumbled, "he listens to me and stays gone." Jeff hopped in his car and pulled out, heading for Braintree, a town neighboring

Boston Craig and his family had moved to a few years prior. As he moved through the midmorning traffic and headed out of the city, his mind raced uncontrollably with one frenetic thought after the next.

What the hell's happening? Who are these people and what do they want with me? Why me? I didn't—why did I do this? Why did I go to that hotel room with Jessica? What the fuck was I thinking? Eden, I'm so goddamn sorry, I—what am I going to do? What does Hope want? And what's with that creepy video? How could he and that other guy have been in the room? How could they—and the whole bit about dialing the phone and then mine ringing was obviously meant to frighten me and make it all seem—but no, it's not even possible, none of this is. I would've seen them in the room, they—did they alter the tape maybe? There are all sorts of programs now where you can—I—wait—did they drug me? Could Jessica have drugged me, put something in my breakfast maybe? Did I leave the table at any point? No, I didn't, I—could she have slipped something in my juice or coffee or—no—this is crazy. It's all a setup. I've been the mark from the start, but why? None of it makes any sense. For Christ's sake, I'm a salesman, what could they possibly want with me?

Just moments from the city, Jeff soon found himself barreling through the streets of Braintree. He'd tried calling Craig's cell and home phones to let him know he was coming and needed to talk, but both went directly to voicemail, so he could only hope he was home and had simply missed the calls.

When Jeff turned at the top of Craig's street he was relieved to see his car parked in front of the house, a modest raised ranch in a quiet working-class neighborhood. As he pulled in alongside Craig's car, he noticed Katy, Craig's wife, was in the passenger seat, and their two kids were in the back.

He waved. Katy returned it with an awkward, embarrassed, almost apologetic wave of her own then looked away as Jeff pulled into their driveway and stepped from the car.

Lugging a suitcase, Craig stumbled out the front door of the house. He froze when he saw Jeff. "What are you…what are you doing here?" he asked, voice shaking. He looked back in the direction Jeff had come, as if expecting someone else to pull in behind him.

"I need to talk." Jeff hurried across the small lawn. "I'm in trouble."

"I can't." He locked the door and checked the street again, his face a tapestry of panic and fear. Of average height, with dark red hair and a matching mustache, Craig normally possessed an extremely laid-back demeanor, but he was clearly terrified, something had frightened him beyond anything Jeff had ever before witnessed. "We're going away for a few days before I start the new job."

"Did you hear what I just said?" Jeff blocked his way. "I need to talk to you, man. I'm in some serious shit."

"Yeah, I…" Craig nervously ran a hand up over his face, across the top of his head and down to the back of his neck. "I gathered, but I can't."

"You *gathered*?"

"Just leave me out of it. This has nothing to do with me."

"What happened? What's wrong with you?"

"Look, whatever it is you're mixed up in, I want nothing to do with these people. I want no part of this."

Fear crawled up Jeff's back and nested at the base of his skull. Hope and his people were going after his friends now? This was insane. How did they even know about Craig?

The application…the reference…

"I don't believe this," he muttered. "This cannot be happening."

Craig tried to get around him then thought better of it. "I don't know what you've gotten yourself into—and I don't want to know—just leave me alone, OK?"

"*Leave you alone*? What the hell are you talking about? Did someone threaten you? What happened?"

"Please, I've got to get out of here."

"Tell me what happened."

Craig's mouth twitched uncontrollably. "I have a wife, I—I've got kids." He leaned closer. "*Children*, you hear me?"

"Who frightened you like this? What did they do? I need to know."

"I can't talk to you, I—they could be watching right now, they—they told me they were watching."

"Who did?"

"You tell me. What's wrong with you? You're *working* with these people? I know times are tough but—"

"No, I'm working with you, remember?"

Craig tried to shoulder by. "I have to go."

"Hey," Jeff said, grabbing his arm. "I *am* working with you, right?"

"They told me you worked for them. I'm not about to interfere with that."

"I need that job, Craig, don't—"

"Goddamn it!" He yanked his arm free, dropped the suitcase and squared his stance. "I didn't want a scene in front of Katy and the kids. Just let me go before this gets out of hand."

"What are you going to do, hit me? You're my best friend."

"Get out of my way, Jeff. Please."

"I need your help. I've got nowhere else to turn."

"They said they'd hurt my family. My *family,* do you understand?"

"Jesus Christ," he sighed, hands on his head. "I'm sorry, I never meant for any of this to touch you. I fucked up. Bad. Real bad. I got into something I didn't mean to and—I don't even understand what's happening myself or how you got involved, but—"

"I'm not involved." He picked up the suitcase. "I'm sorry too. I really am. But you're on your own on this one."

Jeff watched as Craig walked to the car, tossed the suitcase in the trunk then slid behind the wheel and pulled away. He never looked back.

After a brief flirtation with calling the police and taking his chances with Hope delivering a copy of the disc to Eden, Jeff found himself standing on the curb in front of the brownstone where he'd been interviewed. Again, but for the burned-out shell at the end of the block, there were no other cars or signs of life, and the entire area seemed eerily quiet.

He climbed the steps, moved through the door, past the foyer and stopped at the reception area. As before, the desk was unoccupied, the odd sound of a dripping faucet echoed from somewhere deep within the building, and the empty plastic chairs lined the narrow hallway to his right. But this time the first office door was open, as if in anticipation of his arrival. Jeff swallowed hard. Except for the meeting table and two chairs, the office was empty. No coffeemaker, no donuts, no clipboard with application. Clearly he was alone. Why then did he have the overwhelming feeling he was being watched? Skin crawling, he forced himself into the office, sat in the first chair and watched the closed door on the opposite wall. They knew he was here, Jeff was sure of it. They were just making him squirm, letting him twist in the wind a while at the end of his noose, and probably enjoying it.

After several moments, the door opened and Foster Hope entered. This time his presence was intimidating. No longer was he simply an eccentric and elderly businessman, but something far more sinister. He was dressed in the same cream-colored suit as the day before, and Jeff imagined him having dozens of identical outfits hanging in a closet somewhere. The old man acknowledged him with a polite nod. "Good morning, Jeff."

"Why are you doing this to me? Who are you people?"

"I've done nothing to you." He slid into the other chair and crossed his legs. "These are decisions you've made to—"

"What did you do to Craig? He was terrified out of his mind. I've never seen anyone so frightened. Why would you threaten his family, his *children*?"

"I simply had an associate pass along some useful information to him, so he could make an informed decision."

Jeff's hands clenched into fists but he kept them in his lap. The urge to strangle the old bastard was overwhelming. "This is all just some sort of sick game to you, isn't it?"

The look in Hope's emerald eyes indicated he was thoroughly enjoying himself. "*Sick* seems rather harsh, but otherwise, yes, that's exactly what it is. Life is a game, Jeff, and we're all players of one sort or another."

"These aren't just my decisions then. You're manipulating things, forcing me into corners where I have no other way out."

"There are always other ways out of any situation. We all move through the world and do what we have to do in order to survive and flourish. We look out for our best interests, and in the end we make our own decisions." The green eyes narrowed. "Regardless of what I've done or haven't done, you don't *have* to be here. You've chosen to be here."

"Why would you want me to work for you under these conditions? Why would you videotape me with Jessica and—how the hell were you in that room without my knowing it? You and that other…man."

"I often hide in plain sight, Jeff. I find it most effective."

Jeff sat forward with an intense stare of his own, hands flat on the table between them. Despite the heat outside, the room was cool to the point of being nearly cold. Why then was he perspiring so? And how was the temperature so low when there were no fans and appeared to be no air-conditioning? Like everything else, none of it made any sense. "What do you want from me?"

"I'd like to hire you on as a negotiator."

"No, you're forcing me to work for you."

"You have every right to decline at any time. Have I chained you to that chair? Have you been restrained or in any way prevented from leaving? You can get up and walk out of here whenever you like. No one will attempt to stop you, no one will object. We'll part as friends."

"*Friends*? Friends don't blackmail and deceive each other."

"They don't?" Mr. Hope smiled with his large, brilliantly white false teeth. "Jeff, what most people fail to realize in their narcissism and selfishness is that they're not always players in their own games, but often in someone else's."

"So it's your game then," Jeff said, pawing sweat from his forehead.

"Not necessarily."

"Then what are you saying?"

"That you might want to consider it may not be yours either."

Jeff couldn't tell if there was literal meaning in what Hope was saying or if the old man was simply playing with him, so he dismissed his enigmatic musings and tried to focus on what he needed to do to bring the meeting to some sort of conclusion. He'd begun sweating like a stuck pig and needed to get out of there and away from this man. "If I agree to this...*job*...do I have to kill anyone?"

"Certainly not." Hope frowned dramatically. "How absurd."

"If I have to hurt anyone, I won't do it." Jeff drew a deep breath, and despite his fear, looked him in the eye. "So if that's what this is about you can go ahead and deliver a copy of that disc to Eden and I'll just hope she can forgive me for being so stupid."

Hope folded his hands and placed them on the table. No bone-white talons, just manicured fingernails and a gold ring with a large ruby on the middle finger of his left hand. Had he worn that last time? "I'm offering you a position as a negotiator."

"Do I have to do anything illegal?"

"You don't *have* to do anything at all."

"How much do I get paid?"

"I've told you," he sighed, "enough to grant you financial freedom."

"I'd like an actual figure."

"It's hard to put a price on one's happiness, Jeff. Don't you think? Trust me when I tell you it will be a sum beyond anything you're expecting."

"And the discs?"

"What about them?"

"If I come to work for you, I want them turned over to me."

"Once you've completed your trial assignment successfully you and I will decide whether or not your continued employment here is the right move for both parties. Either way, the other copy of the disc, along with the original, will be yours to do with what you like. I'll certainly no longer have any use for them."

"How do I know I can believe you?"

Mr. Hope's eyelids nearly closed, giving him a decidedly reptilian appearance. "You don't."

"After the trial assignment, if I choose to no longer work for you, I can walk away free and clear? Even if you want me to continue?"

"That is correct. I will accept and respect your decision at that point. And of course I'll expect you to accept and respect mine."

"And you and your people will stay away from my family and friends?"

"Of course, I don't involve myself in situations where I'm not welcome."

Jeff looked away and nodded. "All right."

"You're accepting the position then? We officially have a deal?"

"We do."

"I need you to say the words, Jeff."

He bit his tongue until the anger and humiliation had weakened. "I am accepting the position," he finally responded. "We officially have a deal."

"How exciting." Foster Hope pulled a business-sized envelope from his inside jacket pocket and grinned like a demon. "Then let's get to work."

Behind them, through the still open door, the incessant sound of a dripping faucet continued to echo, and from the far end of the hallway came what Jeff guessed was someone shuffling their feet as they walked, accompanied by occasional indecipherable voices, muffled and hushed. Somewhere in the building were others—Jessica, the mousy Ms. Gill and the tall man among them, he was sure—but there was something more…something menacing. He could feel it. Sorrow…pain…fear…all of it palpable and thickening the very air he breathed.

"There's a young man I had some business dealings with a few months ago," Hope explained, his voice bringing Jeff back. "He agreed to pay me for certain services we provided, but when it came time to settle his account he double-crossed me. We're relatively certain he's here in the city, or at least he was as of this morning, but we're not entirely sure where."

"So what do you want me to do?"

"You're to find this man and convince him that it's in his best interest to live up to his end of our business deal."

"If you and your people can't find him, how am I supposed to?"

Hope stared at him dully. "I never said we couldn't find him."

Jeff sighed, stomach churning. "What's the deal you had with him?"

"That's between us." A bright chalky smile returned to his face. "Professional discretion, you understand."

"Mr. Hope, how am I supposed to convince him to do something if I have no idea what it is he's supposed to do?"

"*He* knows, Jeff. Your job is to simply convince him to come to me and do the right thing. To reopen our talks so that we can resolve these matters quickly and efficiently."

"Sounds like something you'd be more than capable of handling yourself."

"It is, but he's refused to return my attempts to contact him. So this is a perfect first assignment for my newest negotiator."

"OK, then how do *I* find him?"

Foster Hope nodded rather formally, as if to agree that the initial phase of their conversation had ended and it was time to move on to other things. He placed the envelope on the table and slid it over to Jeff. "Inside you will find information containing the man's name, his wife's name and their last known address. Far as we know the wife still lives there. He may as well but we can't be sure at this point. Inside the envelope you'll also find a private telephone number where I can be reached once the job has been completed, successfully or otherwise. You will call me at that number, you will be paid immediately thereafter and then we will both make our decisions regarding your future here."

Jeff left the envelope where it was. "And what if I can't find this guy, much less convince him to contact you?"

"Then you fail. But I believe that if you use your intelligence, instincts and skills as a salesman, you'll be able to persuade him to do the right thing, the *honorable* thing." He carefully combed a renegade strand of snow-white hair back from his forehead with a finger. "In all honesty, this is an easy assignment compared to most. Don't want to give you too tall an order right out of the gates, especially without any formal negotiator training."

"And I do this alone?"

"I am many things, Jeff. A fool is not one of them. Of course you'll be *observed*, but you will work alone." He arched an eyebrow. "Unless you feel you need supervision, in which case, I'd be more than happy to have Ms. Bell accompany you."

Jeff felt his face flush. "No, I…"

"I thought not," Hope said, laughing lightly. "This entire matter shouldn't take more than a day to accomplish, so I want you to begin work tomorrow."

"Why not right away?"

"Tomorrow morning. No sooner."

Don't argue. Agree to the conditions and get the hell out of here. "OK."

"But I'll expect to hear from you no later than tomorrow evening."

Nodding, Jeff picked up the envelope.

"Any longer than that and I'll have no choice but to assume something's gone wrong, and then I'll have to come looking for you." The old man was no longer laughing, his eyes no longer sparkling. "And you don't want that, Jeff, do you understand?"

"Yes," he answered tensely, "I do."

"Then I look forward to hearing from you. Until then, good day to you."

Hardly.

8

At nightfall the city was still unbearably hot. After dinner Jeff collapsed into his favorite recliner and attempted to watch a baseball game but was unable to concentrate. The conversation he'd had with Mr. Hope replayed again and again in his mind, and although the entire scenario seemed fantastic at best, he realized all too well just how real this situation was. Clearly there was an illegal, underhanded and dangerous aspect to this whole thing, but if the pay was in cash, no one would know and he could walk away once he was done, he had no choice but to take the risk. What was the alternative? Letting his wife see him in that hotel room with Jessica?

He knew he'd been infuriatingly aloof since Eden had gotten home from work, but he couldn't talk to her about what was taking place. The only way for her to remain safe was to know nothing about any of this.

She wandered in from the bedroom wearing only a long t-shirt. "You OK?"

"I'm fine, honey." *God how I love her,* he thought. *What the hell was I thinking?* The guilt was so strong he couldn't even look at her.

"You sure?"

"Yeah, just a little tired."

"When I left for work this morning everything was great, but since I got home you've barely spoken to me and you're moping around like you got some bad news or something. Is there a problem with the new job?"

"Everything's fine."

"You're not acting like everything's—"

"I just said everything's fine, didn't I?"

"Then why are you in such a *lovely* mood?"

"I'm sorry, I…" He forced a smile, aimed the remote at the TV and switched it off. "I told you, I'm just a little tired, OK? No biggie. Everything's fine with the new job and everything else. I love you."

"Love you, too." She sighed, and then as if she'd just remembered, jerked a thumb at the window and said, "Hey, he's not out there tonight."

Jeff's mind was so far away it took him a moment to realize who she was talking about. "I had a chat with him. I doubt he'll be coming around anymore."

Eden sat on the edge of the recliner. "What did you say to him?"

"I told him to stay the hell away from us and the building."

"Jesus, Jeff." She scooped up a magazine from the coffee table and began fanning herself with it. "That's awfully severe, don't you think?"

"Who gives a shit? He's a bum, for Christ's sake."

"Oh how charming." Eden tossed the magazine aside. "So warm and kind, you know? Why do you have to be so cruel to him?"

"What the hell is it with you and this guy?"

"What are you talking about?"

Jeff stood up. "Why are you so interested in him? It's constant."

She watched him a moment then began to laugh. "Are you *jealous*?"

"What is your fascination with him?" She balked, but he could tell he'd hit a nerve. "There are lots of homeless people in the city, why is *he* so special?"

"I'm a compassionate person, sorry if that offends you."

"No, there's more to it and you know it."

"Oh no, you found out!" she said, eyes wide. "We're fuck buddies!"

"You think this shit's funny?"

"Yeah," she said, laughing again, "I do, actually."

He waved her off. "OK, whatever, no sense in discussing it then."

"I don't know what your problem is tonight," she said, "but I find deliberate cruelty revolting. Especially in someone I love. I'm going to bed. Goodnight."

"Wait, I—look, I don't mean to be cruel, OK? I'm sorry, you know I'm not really like that, it—it's just that I've got other things to worry about right now. I'm focused on *us*, on *our* life. I've been under a lot of stress lately and—"

Someone in the lobby downstairs buzzed their apartment. With Jeff following close behind, fearful it might be Hope or one of his associates, Eden went to the intercom just inside the front door and pressed the button. "Yes?"

"Eden!" a man's frantic voice answered. "Let me in! Please, let me in!"

"I'll be a sonofabitch." Jeff recognized the voice immediately. "You have *got* to be kidding me."

"Please Eden! You can help me, please—*please*—help me, let me in!"

She glanced guiltily at Jeff, unsure of what to say. "Please! Let me in! I don't belong out here!"

"I'm sorry," she said softly. "I can't."

When the intercom fell silent, Jeff ran for the bedroom and looked out the window. The homeless man had already begun to drift down the street, looking back over his shoulder at the apartment every few steps.

When Jeff turned from the window he found Eden standing behind him in the doorway. "How the hell does he know your name?"

She sat at the foot of the bed, hands in her lap. "When I left for work this morning he was out on the steps. He told me his name was Ernie Graham, so I told him my name too, all right?"

"No, it's not all right. Are you insane?"

"I can't believe you're acting like this. It's ridiculous."

"Not gonna argue that one with you. The guy just buzzed our apartment and expected you to let him in. If that doesn't qualify as ridiculous nothing does."

"I said *no* didn't I?"

"Eden, listen to me. We know nothing about this man. He

could have a criminal record, he could be dangerous. Do you understand?"

"Yes, I'm familiar with English. Stop talking to me like I'm a child."

Jeff steadied himself. *Breathe…stay calm…* "I know you mean well and you're only trying to be kind, OK? I get it. But you don't make friends with deranged homeless guys that live on the front steps of the building."

"He's not deranged."

"How do you know?"

"OK, I admit I have sort of a soft spot for him." She threw her arms in the air. "He just—I don't know what it is—I know it sounds crazy but it's almost like I know him somehow. For some reason I feel *especially* sorry for him. Maybe it's some sort of spiritual connection, or a higher power is trying to tell me something, who knows?"

He stared at her, mouth gaping.

"He's just a lost soul, Jeff, not a serial killer."

"This isn't like feeding a stray cat, Eden. It's a little more complicated."

"Have you ever actually spoken with him? Not spoken *at* him, not *threatened* him, but actually spoken with him like you would anyone else?"

"What's your point?"

"He's down and out and hurting. Look around the city. The homeless are everywhere, just like you said. But have you really *seen* them? A lot are women and children. Are they all deranged, too? Are they all criminals? They're just people that have fallen on hard times. If you hadn't gotten that job we eventually would've ended up out there with them. Are we criminals? Are we scum? Are we deranged? All Ernie's looking for is a little compassion and understanding, enough to let him know he still matters and that at least *some* of us care about him and others out there like him."

"Well it's good to know that's all *Ernie's* looking for. I love it, my wife and the bum that lives on our street are on a first-name basis."

"I had a civil conversation with him that lasted all of a minute."

"During which you told him your name and apparently our apartment number. Was there any other personal information you felt compelled to share with your new best bud?"

"If because of my kindness he took it upon himself to buzz the apartment that's not my fault. It's probably not even his. We have no idea what it's like to be out on those streets night after night. We have no idea what that man's been through. Maybe he broke down. Maybe he just wanted to spend one night indoors and was making a crazy plea to—"

"There are shelters in the city, let him go to one of those."

"For his sake I hope he finds one with a free bed."

"Well if not we can always put good ole Ernie up on the couch, right?"

Glaring at him, she yanked the sheet back from the bed with an angry tug and fired a pillow at him. "Nope, you'll already be on it."

"Are you serious?"

"Goodnight Jeff."

Pillow clutched to his chest, he returned to the den and flopped onto the couch. "Yeah," he mumbled, "like I need this shit tonight."

Fine, he thought. Bright and early tomorrow morning he'd get this job done, get paid, make it right with Eden and put this nightmare behind him.

There are no nightmares.

Jeff closed his eyes, but it failed to silence the whispers from his dreams.

There is only the torment of darkness.

9

The following morning, Jeff hailed a cab. He didn't know what to expect and didn't want his car to be identified later if something went wrong. The address scrawled on a small sheet of paper inside the envelope listed an address located in a rough neighborhood in Chelsea, a small city just outside Boston located on the far side of the Mystic River. It also listed the name of the man in Mr. Hope's debt: Stephen Wychek. Jeff had been through Chelsea but knew no one there and was unfamiliar with the layout. Thankfully the driver was able to find the address, a rundown two-story tenement on a relatively quiet street. But even in daylight, the area looked somewhat threatening. "Wait for me," he told the cabbie. "Keep the meter running, I'll only be a few minutes."

As Jeff stepped out of the taxi and approached the tenement steps he saw a faded lace curtain move in one of the windows facing the street. He hesitated, looked around. But for a lone elderly woman carrying a bag of groceries farther down the block, the street was empty. He continued up the steps to the front door, opened it and slipped into a foyer. The walls were cracked, the paint chipped and peeling, and a repugnant odor he couldn't identify hung in the air.

He glanced down at the paper. Alongside the address were the words: *First floor.* Jeff knocked. No one answered, but he could hear movement inside the apartment, so he knocked again. After a moment, a shuffling sound indicated someone had moved up closer to the door.

"Hello?" he said, leaning closer. "Hello?"

From behind the door came a female voice; nervous and muffled. "What do you want?"

"I need to speak to Mr. Wychek."

"He's not here."

"Are you Mrs. Wychek?"

"What do you want?"

"My name's McGrath. I need to speak to Mr. Wychek, it's very important." Jeff looked at the dark stairway leading to the second floor. It was filthy and strewn with garbage. "Could you open the door please?"

"I don't know you."

"Ma'am, please, my name is Jeff McGrath and—"

"What do you want with my husband?"

"I need to speak with him about some personal business."

"What kind of personal business? If this is about the car payment the bank already did a repo, came and took it a couple nights ago."

"It's not about the car."

"What bill's it about?"

"It's not about any bill, I—"

"Then what do you want?"

With a sigh, Jeff rubbed his eyes. This was ludicrous. He obviously wasn't going to get anywhere without turning up the heat. "Ma'am, I need to speak to your husband, understand? Now if he's not home I need you to tell me where I can find him. This is very important. I'm not playing games."

"Get out of here or I'll call the cops."

Jeff thought a moment. "I don't think Foster Hope would appreciate that."

After a lengthy pause he heard locks disengaging. The door opened slowly, but only a crack, the security chain catching. Through the opening, a middle-aged woman with bleary eyes and a drawn face peeked out at him. Her hair was mussed and unwashed, her skin pale and unhealthy looking, and she looked as if she hadn't slept in days. She also looked deeply frightened. Her eyes were filled with tears and her lips trembled like a scolded child's. "Please," she whispered, "please, we…I didn't know, I…"

"It's all right," he said, holding his hands up in an effort to calm her. "I'm not going to hurt you or cause you any trouble. I just need to speak to Stephen."

"Please," she hissed, shaking as tears streamed her face. *"Please."*

Jeff forced a swallow. "Tell me where he is. I only want to talk."

"We have kids," she said, choking on her tears. "Please, I—"

"I want to help your husband, do you understand? Tell me where I can find him and I'll do everything I can to help him make this right with Mr. Hope."

Her watery eyes seemed to focus for the first time, and her mouth fell open. "You don't...You don't know what's happening, do you?"

Jeff looked around nervously, as if expecting to find Hope in the shadows, watching him from the top of the stairs. "Look, I don't want to be here, but I don't have any choice. They're making me do this. All I'm supposed to do is talk to your husband and try to convince him to contact Mr. Hope. That's all."

She shook her head, the tears coming faster now. "Do you know why they're doing this? What did he do to you and your husband? What are they doing to me?" Jeff placed his hand against the doorframe to steady himself. "If you know, please Mrs. Wychek, tell me. What's happening? What have we done? Why us?"

She wiped the tears from her cheeks with a shaking hand, but they were quickly replaced. "Sometimes," she said softly, "you don't have to go looking for the Devil. Sometimes he goes looking for you."

Despite the heat, Jeff felt a sudden burst of cold from deep within him. "Is there anything we can do?"

"Pray?" she asked hopelessly, her hand suddenly fingering a gold cross around her neck.

"Where is your husband, Mrs. Wychek?"

"He's not my husband anymore."

"I don't understand."

"You will."

"Can you tell me where he is?"

Her sad and frightened eyes looked to the floor. "Yes," she whispered. "God forgive me...but yes."

Moments later Jeff was back in Boston. There was a slight break in the stifling heat as an enormous bank of storm clouds slowly rolled in off Boston Harbor. The cab moved through the streets between the theater district and Chinatown, then finally pulled onto a side street and lurched to a stop near a vacant lot strewn with garbage and debris. The driver pointed to a rotting shell of an apartment building just beyond the lot. "That's it."

"Crazy," he mumbled, "no one could actually *live h*ere."

"That's the address you gave me. You want me to wait again?"

"No."

Jeff paid him and stepped out. As he crossed the lot thunder rumbled in the distance and a cool breeze provided an unexpected chill. He reached the base of the steps and looked up at the dilapidated, graffiticovered structure. Most of the windows were blown out and the front doors were missing. He glanced around. The neighborhood was deserted.

A drizzle began to fall, startling a congregation of blackbirds perched along the roof into flight. Jeff watched until they disappeared into the dark clouds overhead. He slowly forced himself up the front steps.

As he entered what had once been a lobby his eyes adjusted to the sudden change in light. A variety of lurid smells wafted all around him, and rain trickled in through several cavities in the high ceiling. A timeworn staircase stood to his right. Jeff ascended it cautiously, testing each step with his weight before continuing.

When he reached the top he followed a long hallway filled with garbage and the splintered remains of furniture to the first apartment. The door had rotted from its hinges and collapsed just inside the entrance. He climbed over the door and into an open area. Broken pallets and a few discarded empty crates lay scattered about, and upon seeing him, a covey of plump rats scurried off, seeking refuge in corners or small portals previously gnawed in the decaying walls.

A rustling sound diverted Jeff's attention. A large piece of tattered plastic hung over one of the windows, rippling in the mounting breeze, and on the floor just beneath it sat a pile of spent liquor bottles.

"Hello?" The only reply was the echo of his voice. "Is anyone here?"

"Joint's taken," a voice behind him said suddenly.

Jeff spun round to see a man standing a few feet away. "Jesus," he gasped, trying to catch his breath.

"You scared the hell out of me."

"What do you want?" Keeping a wary distance, the man produced an enormous hunting knife from his belt and brandished it about between them with a slow and threatening arcing motion.

"Take it easy," Jeff said putting his hands up. "I don't want any trouble."

His eyes widened, as if he were losing sight of him. "Who are you?"

It was difficult to tell the man's age. His clothes were soiled and worn, his hair and face needed to be washed and he was clearly exhausted. "McGrath."

"I don't know nobody named McGrath."

"I'm looking for Steven Wychek."

The man stared at him, dumbfounded.

"Are you Mr. Wychek?" Jeff asked, already wondering if he could outrun this man if need be. "Do I have the right person?"

The man slowly lowered the knife to his side. "Nobody knows where I am. How did you find me?"

"Your wife told me you were hiding here."

"My…wife…" His hostility turned to terror. "My God," he muttered. "You…You're one of them."

"No, I'm not, I—I'm caught up in this the same as you." Confused, Jeff continued to hold his hands up to assure the man that he harbored no bad intentions toward him. "A man named Foster Hope hired me, he's forcing me to work for him."

Wychek raised the knife a bit higher, ready to use it if need be.

"That's not necessary, OK?" Jeff smiled nervously. "All I want to do is—"

"Stay where you are."

"I won't come any closer," he said, hoping to mask his own fear with a docile tone. "Relax, OK? Mr. Hope asked me to tell you that it's in your best interest to settle your debt with him and that you should contact him as soon as possible. He just wanted me to deliver that message. That's it."

The man gave a questioning stare. "You don't know what you're into yet, do you?"

"Honestly?" Jeff asked through a sigh. "No. I don't have any idea."

"You will." Wychek moved toward the window, the knife leveled in front of him. "But by then it'll be too late."

Jeff glanced in the direction of the doorway, fairly certain if he made a quick dash for it he could make it outside well ahead of the man. "What do you owe him? What does he want from you?"

"Everything." Wychek slumped a bit, defeated. "And I'm tired of running, McGrath. I'm tired of being afraid."

"Come with me, and I'll get in touch with Mr. Hope. I'm sure we can all sit down and work out an arrangement both of you can live with."

"You crazy or just dumb as a brick?"

"I'm frightened and confused, same as you."

"Funny how it all fits together," he said, as if to himself. "All I wanted was to get out from under my problems, I…I wanted me and my wife to be free from them, you know? My drinking, the drugs, my running around, I—I can't stop, I'm a fuckup, and she—she's a good woman, my wife. Too good for me, she never deserved this. I wanted to get better so we could both be happy…free. He told me he could help us, told me he could make it all come true. But it was a trick. He's a cruel and evil *fuck*."

"Maybe you and I can help each other."

"Ain't no help against his kind."

"He's powerful, rich and plays demented games with people's lives, but he's a man just like you and me."

"No he's not."

"Come with me," Jeff said again. "We'll confront the bastard together and get to the bottom of this."

Wychek hopelessly bowed his head. "You tell Foster Hope I'll see him real soon."

Before Jeff had a chance to respond, Wychek rushed to the window, and with a horrific scream, launched himself through the plastic drape and plummeted to the street below.

A stomach-churning thud followed.

Jeff ran to the window and saw the carcass of an old refrigerator in the alley below. Sprawled across the top was Wychek's broken body. It flopped over like a rag doll, leaving behind a wide red wake as it slid lifelessly to the ground.

Staggering back, Jeff fell to his knees and vomited. When the nausea had left him he forced himself back to his feet and staggered from the room.

Ignoring the now heavy rain and a burning sensation deep in his gut, he crossed the vacant lot at a full run. As he rounded the corner and joined a more congested street he slowed his pace and tried to appear calm.

At the next block he leaned against the corner of a bank, fumbled his cell phone from his belt and frantically punched in the number he'd been given. It was answered on the first ring, but all Jeff heard was heavy breathing. "Hello?" he said, voice breaking. "Hello!"

"Jeff, is that you?" Mr. Hope asked.

"Something terrible has happened!"

"Calm down. What's going on?"

"Wychek's dead," he said, blurting the words but trying to keep his voice down due to the amount of people passing by. "He's dead."

"I want to be certain I heard you correctly. Would you repeat that please?"

"Wychek. Is. Dead."

"Dead, you say?"

Jeff wiped rainwater from his face with his free hand, looked out at the street and pressed the phone tighter against his ear. "*Yes*," he hissed. "He threw himself out a fucking window."

"Excellent work, Jeff."

"What?" Jeff spun back against the building. "Are you out of your mind?"

"You've successfully completed your first negotiation. Unfortunately, I just don't see it working out for you here at *International Facilitator, Inc.* Your lack of enthusiasm in this situation clearly shows you don't possess what it takes to become a permanent member of our team."

"A man is dead!"

"Yes, how marvelous. Be that as it may, I'm afraid I'll have to terminate your employment with us, effective immediately. However, I am a man of my word, Jeff, and I do plan to live up to my end of our bargain. You will be paid for your efforts today, as promised, and the compensation will grant you what you asked for, financial independence. Meet me at the offices and payment will be arranged."

"I don't want your money, I want answers!"

"It's been a pleasure doing business with you." The line clicked and disconnected.

"Mr. Hope? Mr. Hope!" Jeff snapped his phone shut and tried to clear his mind. He was soaked to the bone and his heart was crashing against his chest with such force he was afraid he might actually be having a heart attack. He slumped against the building, and despite his trembling hands, managed to flip open his phone and hit redial.

"The number you have reached is not in service," a pleasant recorded voice announced. "Please check the number and try again."

Jeff closed the phone and dropped it into his coat pocket as he fought back tears of anger, shock, frustration and disbelief. "This isn't…this can't be happening."

He turned, and there on the corner, watching him through the rain, was Ernie Graham.

10

If the sight of Jeff hurrying in his direction alarmed him, Ernie Graham showed no signs of it as he stood statue-still in the downpour. When Jeff was within reach, he grabbed Graham's arm and squeezed tight, not sure if he'd intended to hurt him or if he was only hanging on for dear life. "*You,*" he snarled. "What do you know about these people?"

He stared at him dully. "What people?"

"Don't fuck with me." Jeff turned and started them both down the street, hand still clamped on Graham's arm. "You told me to stay away from Jessica Bell. You said you heard things, saw things, knew things."

"You're hurting my arm."

"Tough shit, start talking."

"Where are we going?"

As they reached the first alley they'd come to, his question was answered. About halfway through, Jeff spun him around and pushed him against the wall. Ernie slammed the bricks, grimaced and began to cough.

"It didn't have to be you!" Graham said. "It could've been somebody else!"

"What does that mean?"

He doubled over and coughed harder until he hacked up a big ball of phlegm. "It didn't have to be you," he said again, spitting it out. "You could've been kinder to me, you—"

"I tried to be kind to you."

"No," he said, wiping his mouth, "you tried to get rid of me."

"What do you have to do with all this?"

"Your wife, she was kind to me. Eden was kind. Eden *is* kind."

"I told you to leave my wife out of it. Eden has nothing to do with this."

He laughed, his chest gurgling. "Wouldn't you say she's your life?"

Jeff hadn't expected the question, and it took him a moment to answer it. "Yes, of course."

"Then she has everything to do with it."

"She doesn't even know anything's happened."

He nodded in agreement. "And she never will."

"Tell me what you know." Jeff raised his fists. "Or so help me I'll beat it out of you."

"I'm not the one you need answers from. Talk to Hope."

"Who is he? Who is he really?"

"I don't know." Ernie's bloodshot eyes blinked rapidly in the rain. "I only know he's using magic…black magic…whole lot of black magic."

"You can't really believe that."

"You'll believe it soon enough." He smiled his brown-toothed smile.

Jeff brought his hands to his head, ran them through his drenched hair.

"Could be you already do," Ernie went on, "but you're just too scared to admit it."

"What do you mean when you say it didn't have to be me?"

"You'll understand…eventually."

"No," Jeff said, lunging for his throat and pinning him back against the alley wall. "No, you're gonna tell me now."

Ernie struggled to break free but couldn't. "You're choking me, I—I can't breathe!"

"Tell me what you meant, you fuck!"

"You should've stayed away from them like I told you," he said, gagging. "If you did they would've found somebody else and none of this would've touched you or your life."

"How are you involved in this? Are you in on this with them?" He choked him even harder. "Are you one of them?"

"No," he gasped.

Jeff released him. Ernie's legs gave out and he slid slowly to the ground, finally plopping down on his behind in the middle of a puddle. He crawled onto his hands and knees and struggled to get up but didn't seem to have the strength. The rain kept coming, pounding them down. "I'm just a man," he said, weeping suddenly. "I made some mistakes but I'm a good person. Why do I have to live like some piece of trash in the street? I don't deserve this. I never hurt anyone. What did I ever do to anybody? What did I ever do to you?"

Ashamed, Jeff looked away.

He punched the ground, splashing at the puddle with his fist as his body bucked with emotion. "No one gives you anything in this life! You have to take it! Even if you don't want to, there's no other way! Life leaves us no choice but to rip it away from somebody else so we can have ours! It's the nature of things, *our* nature!"

"No. It's a lie someone like Foster Hope relies on us believing, because without it he's powerless." Jeff stumbled away, head spinning.

When he reached the mouth of the alley, he looked back. Ernie Graham was on his knees, head back and hands reaching for the sky as if to grab hold of something only he could see, some sliver of peace and salvation perhaps, promised by veiled and forgotten gods no longer believed in, safely hidden away in storm clouds and concealed by a relentless rain.

Nothing seemed real anymore. The world took no particular notice. It just kept churning, bustling all around him as he moved through the city streets, another lost soul barely cognizant of the driving rain. All he could think about was Foster Hope, those horrible emerald eyes, the white hair, the lined face, the big false teeth, and then he'd fade to black and Steven Wychek would take his place, terrified but surrendered to the inevitable as he launched himself through the plastic-covered window and plummeted to the alley below.

The brownstone…

Jeff stood across the street. If they'd already vacated the building he certainly wouldn't have been surprised. He'd actually expected to find it empty. Regardless, he'd been drawn there. He'd dismissed his desire to simply return home or go to Eden's office and take her out of there and explain to her what was happening and why together they needed to leave the city and go somewhere else, to put this madness behind them like the bad dream it was and move on with their lives. They'd find jobs, a safe place to live in a quiet little town, maybe have a couple kids and have real lives, real love…peace…

He crossed the street, climbed the steps and tried the door. It opened.

Once inside, he continued on to the reception area, his eyes slowly adjusting to the lack of light and bringing everything into eventual focus. The sound of rain softened, but the same annoying dripping sound echoed along the hallway. It smelled musty and old here, as if nothing alive had moved within these walls in a very long time. Rather than going into the meeting room, this time he followed the hall to the rear of the building instead.

Like a tunnel, the dark hallway turned and emptied into a large open room that looked almost like some sort of old ballroom. It was large, with high ceilings, no interior walls, old hardwood floors, plaster walls and a ceiling marred with age and littered with spider web cracks. Void of furniture, it was completely empty but for someone kneeling in the center of the room, rocking slowly in the shadows. He couldn't be sure if it was a man or woman, as they were wrapped from head-to-toe in a sheer dark cloak, like an ancient burial shroud.

Jeff remained in the doorway. The person's whispers, the cadence like prayers or chants, bled across the open space, but they seemed unaware of his presence. Even when the familiar clacking sound of heels hitting the floor broke the silence and Jessica Bell entered the room from a door on the far wall, the person continued rocking, head bowed and undeterred.

As she crossed the room in her business suit, towing a suitcase on wheels behind her, he saw her nude and atop him in the hotel room, her breasts wet with perspiration, her hair a tangled mess, her legs tight against his hips as she bucked and rode him, her hands pressed flat against his chest and her eyes wild and alive and burning with the crazed passion and fire of a woman possessed.

She stopped a few feet from him, looking almost pleased to see him. "Jeff," she said, "what are you doing here?"

"What do you think I'm doing here?"

Jessica smiled, and he felt himself stir. "Same as the others, looking for answers you won't find, not here anyway."

"Why do you do these things to people?" He struggled even now to resist her, but the woman dripped sex. Disgust filled him. There, with the lust. "Why are you a part of this?"

"Like the card says, we're just facilitators."

"Of what?"

"Human frailty."

"But why?"

"Why not?"

"What do you possibly gain from all this?"

Her arrogance resembled that of any great predator, one completely confident in its invulnerability. "You can't figure out if you want to fuck me or kill me with your bare hands," she purred. "Deep down, you want to do both. Don't let it tear you up. Truth is neither of us can help it. A mouse to cheese or a moth to flame, it's no different. It's the way we're wired."

"Does that help you sleep at night?"

"I suppose it would if I slept at all."

Jeff ignored his fear and motioned to the shrouded person with his chin. "Who is that?"

"Doesn't matter, aren't you here to see Mr. Hope?"

He nodded.

She cocked her head toward the far side of the room and the door she'd come through. "Afraid I can't stay, got a plane to catch. Things to do, people to see. Business is booming. But then, our business is *always* booming." Jessica winked, strolled by him then stopped. "If it makes you feel any better," she said without looking back, "it was never really about you."

The sound of her footfalls and the plastic suitcase wheels rolling along the floor resumed then grew fainter until they too fell silent, as if absorbed by the building itself. All that remained was whispers and the incessant dripping.

Jeff walked across the large, open, windowless room, taking a wide path around the shrouded figure. But when he was within reach, the woman—he could tell now that it was female—jerked her head up from prayer. The cloak slipped free of her head and fell down around her neck, revealing a hideously pale and sunken face, the skin so withered it seemed nearly mummified. Where her eyes should've been were two empty black sockets, remnants of blood and fluid still staining her cheeks like war paint. Horrified, Jeff took a step back.

The woman's lips—thin, taut and bloodless—parted and her whispers became a frail voice. "Is someone there?"

It was impossible to tell how old she was, but the woman was more than likely middle-aged. Or had been…

"Are you there?" she asked, hands reaching out in darkness. "I can…I can hear someone…please… won't you help me?"

Jeff swallowed. Hard. "I don't know what to do."

The woman's head swiveled back and forth, trying to pinpoint the exact location of his voice. "Please, they've left me here and I don't know what's happening. There's been some sort of mistake, I…I've been praying but…"

Jeff brought a trembling hand to his mouth. A pair of black glasses with unusually thick lenses lay at the woman's feet. "Ms. *Gill*?"

"Yes," she said, nodding furiously. "Do I…Do I know you?"

"What has he done to you?"

"I don't know, but I can't *see*. Please…" Her withered hands reached for him again, the fingernails torn free and the skin beneath sewn closed with thick leather-like thread. The far door creaked as it opened slightly. Jeff and the woman both turned toward the sound, but she began to groan in horror as she fell to her side and curled into a fetal position. "No, oh—oh no—don't…"

A scratchy sound echoed through the room from just beyond the door, a stylus dropped into the groove of an old record album. A keyboard intro was followed by a haunting guitar riff, and as the eerie vocals kicked in, Jeff realized someone was blasting Iron Butterfly's classic rock epic *In-A-Gadda-Da-Vida.*

Jeff headed straight for it, stopping just before the cracked door. He reached out and pushed, swinging the door open wider. The music, deafening now, spilled out from a turntable and stereo system inside the narrow room. Standing in the shadows was the tall man. Dressed in the same black suit, white shirt and skinny black tie, he seemed oblivious to Jeff's presence, stood pencil-straight and swung his long arms up and down to the beat of the song, above his head then down behind his back in slow arcing motions, snapping his fingers and lolling his back and forth as if his neck had broken. The look of abject sorrow he'd had prior was gone, replaced with a blank, emotionless expression. Eyes closed, he continued to dance, arms swinging. Jeff noticed a desk against the wall to the man's right, a cloth spread out across the top upon which numerous items had been placed. A closer look revealed a neat row of various medical utensils and instruments of torture and mutilation. Most were pristine and shiny silver, but a few were stained with blood and other fluids, as well as small chunks and slivers of what was probably human flesh.

Sitting just beyond the tall man, in the far corner of the room, was Foster Hope. The old man was slumped in a rickety wooden chair; head bowed and chin touching his chest as if in sleep. He too seemed oblivious to Jeff's presence. Though he wore the same suit and tie, this time he looked different.

Hope's hands, resting in his lap, now resembled those in Jeff's dream, the manicured fingernails replaced with long, thick, bone-white talons that seemed better suited to the paws of a large jungle cat than the hands of a human being. His white hair was a bit mussed but it wasn't until he slowly raised his head and turned to Jeff that the other changes became evident as well.

"Christ Jesus," Jeff whispered.

The old man's eyes were no longer a brilliant emerald. The lenses had been removed and all that remained were solid black orbs, moist, inhuman, disturbing inky pools. His lips parted and curled up into a hideous smile, the large false teeth gone, replaced by bloody, diseased gums he slurped at with a black and forked reptilian tongue.

Jeff felt his legs give out but he caught the edge of the desk at the last moment and leaned onto it, preventing himself from collapsing to the floor. Mind reeling, he stared at Foster Hope, wanting to turn away but unable to, his vision blurring and becoming watery.

Just off the room was a bathroom, the door open. Propped across a shelf above a large sink was a human head, eyes gouged out, mouth slashed wide into a freakish and Joker-like grin. Several others lay in a heap on the dirty tile floor. Blood plopped in a slow, steady rhythm from scraps of flesh that had once been a neck down into the sink, and though the music made it impossible to hear, Jeff now knew the source of the incessant dripping.

Everything in his being told him to run, but his body refused to respond. Shaking, he held tight to the desk until his vision slowly returned to normal.

The tall man fell still. After a moment he noticed Jeff for the first time. Eyes never leaving him, he lifted the arm from the record and the music stopped. The dripping sound returned as he rolled the instruments up in the cloth, tucked them under his arm then strode back out into the large room. The shrouded woman began to scream, and as Jeff looked back over his shoulder he saw the tall man dragging her by her hair across the floor and out into the hallway. He put his hands to his ears and fell across the desk. "Stop it, for—for Christ's sake, stop it!"

The screams grew softer and were eventually silenced. Foster Hope sat grinning and staring at him with his onyx eyes throughout.

Jeff struggled back to his feet, clinging desperately to whatever scraps of sanity he could still claim, and saw that somehow the old man had returned to his previous state. Perhaps he'd never really changed at all. Or perhaps Jeff had only really seen Foster Hope as he truly was for that one horrifying instant.

"So good to see you again, Jeff," the old man said. He rose from his chair and closed the bathroom door, emerald eyes sparkling as he smiled brightly.

"The tapes," he managed.

"There, as I promised." Hope motioned to two unmarked video cassettes on the desk. Next to them was a large wastebasket, a bottle of lighter fluid and a box of matches. "I assumed you'd want to destroy them."

"How do I know these are them?"

He rolled his eyes. "Come on, Jeff, the game's over. You must know that by now. Those are the tapes. You have my word."

"Your *word*? You can't be serious."

The old man's face hardened. "I'm dead serious, boy."

Jeff scooped up the cassettes, pulled the tape free from within them and threw them into the wastebasket. After dousing them with lighter fluid he struck a match and threw it in. The tapes went up quickly, the awful chemical stench of burning plastic cases wafting all about the room.

"And now to the matter of your compensation," Hope said. "You've earned it, and will therefore soon find that I have paid you in full."

Jeff stepped back, closer to the open doorway. "Who are you?"

"Who do you think I am?"

"*What* are you?"

"I have many names." He traced his lips with a finger, the talons still in place, like razors. "Wizard…Necromancer… Djinn…*Sorcerer.*"

"This isn't happening. None of this is real."

"I'm as real as the human capacity for boundless greed and self-interest is. Do you really believe any of the wishes your kind ever have are anything but self-serving?"

"Yes, I do."

"Then you're a fool. And you're weak. But you amuse me, much the way a mouse amuses a cat. I like to play, though I know my games are particularly disturbing to you. But then, that's the whole point, isn't it. Like the cat, I toy with my mice however I like. And when I grow bored I finish them off without remorse or thought or even a hint of compassion." Hope moved closer, relishing the fact that each time he did Jeff took another step back. "Because I am *eternal,* and you are little more than a faded scar on the ass of your so-called God."

"Why me?"

"Run along, little rabbit." Hope shooed him away with his

hands. "You've stumbled into a den of hungry wolves."

The rain brought him back...wet and cold on his flushed face... away from those horrible green eyes, it was suddenly all around him, a tangle of lust, terror, regret, confusion and anger, clinging to him like flypaper. An explosion of faces—memories of people and events, time with no linear meaning but instead a sandstorm of disjointed seconds tumbling through space, a limitless number of possibilities flowing like water—a montage of two lives and the people, places and things that constituted them whirling together as one.

And then, Eden...looking on as one life—his life, her life, their history, love and laughter, tears, hope, disappointments, fears and triumphs—spiraled away into darkness, splintered to smoke and ash... taking her with it while the other life rose to prominence, one of sorrow and heartbreak, failure and neglect. Amidst screams—his and someone else's—Eden was torn from him. And all that remained was the rain and faint traces of laughter. The horrible laughter of something no longer human, disguised as the cackling of a sick old man.

As if awakening from a dream, Jeff realized he was on the street. Fighting back tears of shock and confusion, he leaned against the side of a building, drenched and frightened. "What the hell's happening to me?"

Something hit the wall, not far from his face.

Startled, Jeff pushed away from the building and turned in the direction from which it had come.

A surly-looking police officer tapped the wall next to him with his nightstick. "Come on, keep moving, no loitering. Let's go, move it."

"Officer, there's no problem here, I—"

The cop nudged him with a beefy gloved hand. "Just move along."

"I stopped to make a call." He reached for his cell phone. It wasn't there.

"Uh-huh. I'm not telling you again. Move along." Jeff staggered away, caught his balance then started off down the block. Doing his best not to appear too upset, he purposely moved in a slow, controlled stride, but noticed people were giving him an unusually wide berth. Most looked away as if repulsed. With his discomfort growing, he stopped in front of a large store window to examine his reflection.

Very slowly, he touched his hands to the face staring back at him.

Ernie Graham's face.

11

"My God," he whispered. "What have you done to me?"

Through the constant surge of people moving along the street behind him, he saw Foster Hope emerge with a devilish grin. "You wanted freedom from the rent, credit card bills, car payments—all of it. Your wish was for independence from those things. Now you have it."

"But—"

"Don't worry," Hope told him. "Eden's going to be just fine."

"Eden," he cried, his fingertips scraping down across the stubble on filthy cheeks that were not his own. "She..."

"Ernie Graham once worked for me as well. His wish was for a new life." The old man licked his lips excitedly. "Your life, Jeff."

"No...I..."

"And now I've given it to him."

He continued to stare, transfixed by his reflection and what he knew to be impossible. "God*damn* you."

"Indeed He did," Hope sighed, "a very long time ago."

Jeff turned from their reflections expecting to see Hope standing next to him. But there was no one there. When he looked back at the store window, Hope's reflection had vanished as well.

"He's still out there."

As he sat up, Jeff's perspiration-soaked back peeled away from the bed sheet. He squinted drowsily at the clock on the nightstand. The numbers were a jumbled blur. "Eden?"

"Hey," she said softly. "What are you doing up?"

"I couldn't sleep." Perhaps carelessly, she stood nude at the apartment window. "I needed something cold to drink." She held up a bottle of water in evidence and then ran the cool plastic across her brow and down along her flushed cheek. "It's after midnight and he's still out there."

"Of course he is." Jeff swung his feet to the floor. "That's where he lives."

"It's ridiculous. No one should be living on the streets in this day and age."

Jeff searched the nightstand, located his eyeglasses and slipped them on. "Jesus, get out of the window."

"It's dark, he can't see in."

He sat on the edge of the bed and watched shadows slink along the smooth contours of his wife's back. Glistening with perspiration, her flesh looked like it had been sprayed down with a fine mist. "I was having a dream," he told her. "Just now, it woke me."

"What was it about?"

"I was here, in the city, but I was lost and I couldn't find you. It was like I had no memory of the city at all. I just kept aimlessly wandering the streets looking for you. I looked everywhere, but I couldn't find you."

"It's OK," she said. "I'm right here."

"Yes." He smiled. "You really are right here with me…aren't you?"

"Of course, sweetie." Eden pushed a wisp of short brown hair from her eyes. "Where else would I be?"

What he didn't tell her was that in the dream he'd been running. In a panic of frenzied terror he'd been sprinting through the streets of Boston as if a pack of wild dogs had been right on his heels…or perhaps as if he'd been one of those dogs himself…or something similar…feral and alone and lost in a rage of night, harsh, dangerous and without end.

"And I'm here, too," he said, as if just realizing it, "with you."

She cocked her head, baffled. "Are you still asleep?"

"No. No, I…I'm awake now." He gazed at her beauty. "Come here."

As she started toward him the buzzer for the door downstairs suddenly sounded, startling them both. Eden quickly threw on a lightweight robe and hugged herself, eyeing her husband nervously throughout.

Without a word, they crossed the apartment to the intercom just inside the front door. Jeff stepped aside and nodded for Eden to answer it.

She pressed the button. "Yes?"

"Eden!" a man's frantic voice answered. "Let me in! Please, let me in!"

Jeff recognized the voice immediately but said nothing.

"Please Eden! You can help me, please—*please*—help me, let me in!"

She glanced guiltily at Jeff, unsure of what to say.

"Please! Let me in! I don't belong out here!"

"I'm sorry, Ernie," she said softly. "I can't do that." She switched off the intercom, and together, she and Jeff returned to the bedroom. He slid into bed as she ventured back to the window for the bottle of water she'd left on the sill.

Eden looked at the street two stories below. The homeless man had returned to the base of their steps and gazed up at her, a crippling sorrow filling his eyes. For reasons unknown even to her, Eden felt inexplicably drawn to him ever since he'd first appeared on their street a few days before. She held his stare with an impassive version of her own. She could see his lips moving but couldn't hear what he was saying, just vague whispers in the night.

She closed her eyes.

Behind her, she could hear Jeff slip out of his pajama bottoms, his breath heavy and excited. "Come back to bed, baby."

Eden opened her eyes. The homeless man was gone.

ABOUT THE AUTHOR

Greg F. Gifune is a best-selling, internationally-published author of several acclaimed novels, novellas and two short story collections. Working predominantly in the horror and crime genres, Greg has been called, "The best writer of horror and thrillers at work today" by *New York Times* best-selling author Christopher Rice, "One of the best writers of his generation" by both *The Roswell Literary Review* and horror grandmaster Brian Keene, and "Among the finest dark suspense writers of our time" by legendary best-selling author Ed Gorman. Greg's work has been published all over the world, translated into several languages, received starred reviews from *Publishers Weekly, Library Journal, Kirkus* and others, is consistently praised by readers and critics alike, and has garnered attention from Hollywood. Two of his short stories, HOAX and FIRST IMPRESSIONS have been adapted to film, his novella MIDNIGHT GODS will soon be made into a feature film, and his novel CHILDREN OF CHAOS is under a development deal to be made into a television series. His novel THE BLEEDING SEASON, originally published in 2003, has been hailed as a classic in the horror genre and is considered to be one of the best horror/thriller novels of the decade. Greg resides in Massachusetts with his wife Carol, a few cats and a dog named Dozer. He can be reached online at:

gfgauthor@verizon.net or on Facebook and Twitter.

Visit his official site for updates and info at: https://gregfgifune.wordpress.com/

CROSSROAD
PRESS

www.ingramcontent.com/pod-product-compliance
Lightning Source LLC
Chambersburg PA
CBHW072237190626
46809CB00018B/2715
* 9 7 8 1 9 4 9 9 1 4 7 8 8 *